She's lying in the dry ditch—a girl. Or the ghost of one. I stop breathing and wonder if she has too. Her head's thrown back, and her eyes are closed above the line of her chin. But her neck's straight, unwrenched, and her arms are at her sides, one slightly bent. Her hands in smooth tight leather gloves hold fistfuls of rooted weeds in a grip. A death grip?

RICHARD PECK was born in Decatur, Illinois. He attended Oxford University in England and holds degrees from DePauw University and Southern Illinois University. He is the author of *Secrets of the Shopping Mall*, *Are You in the House Alone?*, *Ghosts I Have Been*, *Through a Brief Darkness*, *Dreamland Lake*, and *Representing Super Doll* (all available in Dell Laurel-Leaf editions). His adult novel, *New York Time*, was recently published by Delacorte Press. Mr. Peck lives in New York City.

ALSO AVAILABLE IN LAUREL-LEAF BOOKS:

SECRETS OF THE SHOPPING MALL, *Richard Peck*

ARE YOU IN THE HOUSE ALONE?, *Richard Peck*

GHOSTS I HAVE BEEN, *Richard Peck*

THROUGH A BRIEF DARKNESS, *Richard Peck*

DREAMLAND LAKE, *Richard Peck*

REPRESENTING SUPER DOLL, *Richard Peck*

THE DREADFUL FUTURE OF BLOSSOM CULP,
      Richard Peck

THE CHOCOLATE WAR, *Robert Cormier*

I AM THE CHEESE, *Robert Cormier*

THE BUMBLEBEE FLIES ANYWAY, *Robert Cormier*

1.25

CLOSE ENOUGH TO TOUCH

Richard Peck

87-20

LAUREL-LEAF BOOKS

LAUREL-LEAF BOOKS bring together under a single imprint outstanding works of fiction and nonfiction particularly suitable for young adult readers, both in and out of the classroom. Charles F. Reasoner, Professor Emeritus of Children's Literature and Reading, New York University, is consultant to this series.

Published by
Dell Publishing Co., Inc.
1 Dag Hammarskjold Plaza
New York, New York 10017

For Ellie and Dwain Dedrick

"Spring and Fall" by Gerard Manley Hopkins
used by permission of Oxford University Press.

Laurel-Leaf Library ® TM 766734,
Dell Publishing Co., Inc.

ISBN: 0-440-91282-2

RL: 5.6

Reprinted by arrangement with Delacorte Press
Printed in the United States of America
September 1982

10 9 8 7 6 5

Chapter 1

Dory and I took a blanket and went down to the pier just after dark. It was Fourth of July night last summer. The pier's about half rotted out, so the blanket was to sit on because of the splinters. But it was a little chilly after sundown, so I pulled the blanket over our shoulders. We sat there, swinging our feet off the end of the pier, waiting for the fireworks display across Juniper Lake. With our arms around each other.

I never can say what I mean, but I had something to say that night, the only time Dory was up at the cottage. And I wanted to get it out before the sky lit up. I needed to say it in the dark, holding her next to me, warm inside the blanket, both of us looking out over the black water. Then if it was the wrong thing to say, I wouldn't have to know it by looking in her eyes. I remembered not to clear my throat first.

"I love you, Dory. I always will."

For maybe a minute the only sound was the lake lapping the pilings and the weedy beach behind us. Then Dory sighed, and I thought: *This is it. I shouldn't have—*

"I love you too, Matt. What took you so long?" Then she tucked her head into the hollow of my shoulder, and the first rocket sizzled up from the far shoreline. A bright, white flower of fire opened over the lake, and embers fell like snow, white all the way to the water. The sky and the little lake were alive like morning. A red, white, and blue daylight broke over and over and higher and higher. The far shore thundered and roared with high explosives. I didn't have to say any more. She couldn't have heard me. I didn't need to say any more. She'd heard.

At the end of the weekend it was just evening when Dory and I started back in the El Camino. I thought there were other things I ought to say in the hour we had, but I didn't know what they were or how to say them. Maybe I'd said all I needed to for now.

Dory sat in the middle of the seat with her shoulder against mine and one of her legs tucked up under her. We watched the first stars come out and then begin to fade as we got closer to the glow of city lights.

The traffic back to town was heavy but steady. My dad and my stepmother had started back early to beat it. But Dory and I had stayed behind to close up the cottage, so we hit the rush: a long chain of red taillights three lanes wide heading south and the spaced white glare of oncoming traffic across the divider. I'd grab little glimpses of Dory to see how the light from the dashboard played on her face.

Then her head settled nearer my shoulder, and there was only the blur of her hair, black in the night.

Then a blue flasher, revolving, signaled a trooper's car somewhere ahead, and the chain of taillights showed redder as they slowed past it. A wreck maybe. We both started looking when the blue flasher was still well ahead.

Then right there on the grass by the highway was a deer—a doe as still as a statue, with her head up and her muzzle only a couple of yards from the traffic. Her legs were folded under her, and every headlight picked up her eyes. She had to be terrified, but it didn't show.

The traffic was backing up, so we moved past the doe at a crawl. "That's incredible," Dory said. "It's beautiful."

Then we were edging past the cop car: a black-and-white pulled just off the slab behind a big Oldsmobile and people standing around, talking to the cops. Past it, I saw in the rearview mirror that one of the Olds's headlights was out.

We were a couple of miles farther on before Dory said anything. "What happened? What did it mean?"

"The deer must have started to make a run across the expressway. The Oldsmobile caught it on its front right side. The headlight was out."

"But the deer," Dory said. "It's okay. It was just sitting there completely calm. Isn't it okay?"

"I don't think so. I think it's crippled."

It was. Nothing could have made a deer stay that close to the light and the noise.

"But they can do something for it, can't they?"

"Yes."

"You mean take it to a vet."

"I don't think so. I think the cops will take care of it."

"I know what you mean. Don't say it."

I wasn't going to. We drove on then, and Dory was crying without making a sound. Out of the corner of my eye I could see the tears on her face.

That was last summer. It's March now, a different year, and I'm going back up to Juniper Lake by myself. It'll never be perfect again, but it's still my place, the only place I can think of to be now.

I've just told Beth where I'm going.

She's standing at the drainboard, dressed for work, drying the coffee maker parts, handling plastic like it's fine china. She isn't looking at me, which is just as well.

"Matt, I don't think I'd go up there today if I were you." She dries her hands a finger at a time, twisting the wedding ring Dad put there.

"You might, Beth, if you were me."

She glances up at the clock over the door and down at my sweatshirt, skimming my face. Still, I see the lost look in her eyes.

I shouldn't be putting her through this. She isn't even old enough to be my real mother. All I can think of to say is, "I'm not going up there to drown myself."

She flinches, brushes a strand of hair off her forehead. I know she's wishing Dad hadn't taken the Duster and gone off to work at the Industrial Park way ahead of his car pool, though I know why he did, and understand.

4

"You could run right here, somewhere." Her voice wobbles, looking for a possibility.

"On the school track? I don't think so."

"No, I suppose not." She turns the ring around and around. "In the park maybe. Or the forest preserve. Somewhere."

"Up at the lake," I say, the car keys to the El Camino jingling in my hand because there's no pocket in my sweat pants.

"You'll be back—"

"In time. I'm just going to run. Not run away."

She looks aside from that. "I'll be taking the afternoon off. So will Lola," she says, naming my grandmother. "And of course your dad."

I don't remember the hour's drive up to the lake, not even the turnoff onto the gravel access road that winds up into the woods past Ritchey's Riding Academy and then loops down by the lake in front of the cottage. I don't remember the drive even when it's happening, if that makes any sense.

But then I'm sitting here in front of the cottage. The car's stopped, and I've killed the engine, and I'm listening to the wind in the branches. The ice is off the lake, even the gray rim at the shoreline down by the pier. I'm out of the car, edging the stuck screen door across the porch floor. The key turns hard in the front door.

On this March day it's still February inside. A sprig of tinsel's still stapled up over the window from the day we spent up here at Christmas. But the rest of the place is in hibernation, waiting for summer. Collapsed aluminum chairs are stacked along the walls, and the redwood picnic bench brought inside for the winter fills up the emptiness.

I automatically flip the switch in my bedroom even though the electricity's off. And grovel around on the closet floor for my Nike shoes I always wear up there at the lake, though I don't need the extra traction on those roads.

Then, when I'm backing out of the closet, I see something wadded in a corner, forgotten from the summer, from the Fourth of July. I reach for it and see the yellow beach towel, musty-smelling and already in my hand. It's time to get out and run then, because the towel's not mine. It was Dory's.

The pipes are drained, so I don't swing by the kitchen for a cup of water, a minor infraction of the runner's rule: Drink before you're thirsty.

Laces knotted hard, I begin to run from the bottom of the porch steps without doing my stretches first. It's cooler in the breeze I make, then warmer. I run—skid down over the pine needles on the rise of the yard. Then I'm running the lakeside lane, hopscotching around the cannonball rocks rolled down in the winter.

I break all the rules, losing power before the rises, throwing my feet and hearing the slap. Each foot falls eight hundred times in a mile, give or take, and I think about counting to focus my mind.

On the rising loop of the road I stagger and feel a flick in my calf. But that's all the pain there is. I've been running all winter, on the school track and in the forest preserve.

Even before I hit the gravel part of the road I know it's no good. Running's the art of tolerating pain, and I'm too toned up to feel it. There isn't enough physical pain. I nearly turn back, or pitch over into the spiky weeds along the white crisscross fence of the riding academy.

But I go on for no particular reason, pulled by the rhythm when my heartbeat and footfalls begin to mesh. I even count them both, off and on, though I know the long, wandering oblong of road is an exact 2.3 miles.

Then I lose count and regain consciousness. I look for one of the whitewashed stones I set in as mile-markers the summer that England's Sebastian Coe broke the mile record at 3:49. And I spot one, still half-white in among the grayer stones.

I've pretty much bleached out my mind in the first half of the run, but I'm coming up to midpoint. It's the fork down to the lake with the row of country-style mailboxes.

And there's the tree I nearly grazed in the car last Fourth of July weekend, when Dory and I were driving back from the Dairy Freeze after the fireworks. I was high on frozen custard that night, and relieved, I guess, because I'd told her what I had to tell her.

My mind blanks, and I run with my eyes on the ground, watching gravel flow under me, each stone a little world. I'm running on an empty stomach. No carbohydrate loading on this trip. But still I'm not light-headed enough. The euphoria, the breaking through isn't happening. I've had some highs on this stretch of road, but what made me think there'd be one now?

Down toward the lake again, running in one rut

and then the other. Shoes graze the mound between, where the flattened black dandelions never give up.

In the first summer I ran, I did all the things: had an old painter's cap crammed with ice cubes to melt as I went, cold and reviving on my face for most of the distance.

I feel ice up there now, or a numbness. My mind begins to skip like my feet—around things. I'm thinking about who I was before Dory. And what I wanted, just over a year ago.

There's nothing there for a minute, and then I begin to remember, mostly trivia.

I was a tenth-grader, your basic kid. Nobody in particular. Still feeling fairly out of it because I hadn't come to town till junior high, and even by then most of the groups were already pretty sewed up.

I was just topping out at six feet tall and trying not to fall down when I ran.

Remembering to use Ban roll-on deodorant every day and shaving every other.

Thinking about boosting myself up to the bottom rung of the honor roll to help lower the insurance premiums once I got my license.

And getting Dad to pop for the '65 El Camino crying out for racing stripes and new vinyl at the back of the "previously owned" Chevy lot. Picking through parts places for four matching hubcap covers and chrome stripping just in case. Getting a part-time job when I turned sixteen to clinch the deal.

And thinking about girls in an abstract way, checking through their postage-stamp pictures in the yearbook. Contrasting these with the full-color of my fantasies.

Somehow it's not enough to remember. I was pretty immature before Dory.

But at least I'm working up a sweat now, which is good. I find my stride again on the last stretch down by the lake. I'm running alone in the woods, in the world. Because Dory's dead.

And I have to get back for her funeral.

Chapter 2

School doesn't close. In January we had some snow days, and there's the usual threat about extending into summer vacation. But friends of Dory's and the choir can be excused early for the graveside service. And the pallbearers of course. I'm one of them.

Five of us are in Dory's class: juniors. The other one's her brother-in-law, from Milwaukee, I think. I've met him a couple of times, but he doesn't remember.

We're standing behind the hearse. Todd Eames, Bill Matlack, Ron Harvey, Jay Rosen, me. Standing around, not making eye contact, glancing toward the brother-in-law for some leadership. He's pinstriped, horn-rimmed, young in adult terms, and the only one of us with an almost black suit.

The gravestones stretch out around us under an enormous sky. It's any suburb's cemetery, probably a farmer's field not long ago, without a tree in it higher than my head. I'm hot and chilled to the bone in the only suit I have, and we stand around waiting behind the tail pipe of the hearse while the long line of cars snakes in through the gates. Cars are stopping out on Dumfries Road now, two blocks away, and their doors are opening. The schoolbus with the choir is lumbering up the narrow cemetery road, with one set of wheels in the ditch.

Let them all take their time. Things can only get worse.

The schoolbus is moving past us now, yellow sidelights blinking, and there's this eerie silence. A schoolbus is its own stereo system: whoops, cheers, animal imitations, arms out windows banging on the side, transistors competing. But today, nothing. Only the muffling of parkas over choir robes.

People are out of the cars and walking along the gully between the gravestones and the road. Looking as far from myself as possible, I make out Beth and Dad faced the other way in the crowd. Gram—my grandmother—is moving up to meet them. She's come straight from work. Her winter coat's pulled tight around the wrapper she wears at the check-out counter.

The funeral directors are moving up ahead of the hearse to the Lincoln limo with the purple pennants where Dory's family sits waiting. Oversize car doors squeak open.

The choir's walking in clumps of three or four toward the grave site. The tails of their robes blend together, black, and still there's this priestly silence about them.

When they get up to the rows of folding chairs

and the tent, they begin to regroup. Altos with altos. Sopranos with sopranos, except for one who isn't there. Tenors behind. Basses, bigger, behind them. Still, I don't know them, singly or as a group.

Miss Burman mounts an imaginary podium—none of this is real. She waves them into place, shifting them a quarter inch one way, then another. There's got to be a baton parked under her arm, because there always is. I look at the filling rows of chairs, the tent with the open side. The flowers, though the family didn't want any sent. People file down the rows, like they were inside somewhere: in church or the auditorium for graduation.

The Gundersons start walking away from the limo. Dory's mother is first, walking away, so I don't have to see her face. She's leaning on the arm of some man I don't know.

Mr. Gunderson walks behind her with his head down and his neck thick above the collar of his topcoat. Beside him is Ruth-Ellen, Dory's younger sister. She's holding his hand, or he's holding hers. Next comes Dory's older sister, Jess.

Behind their incompleteness, other people follow: relatives, people who just appear at times like these.

I watch them until they're up to the front line of chairs. The farther away they get, the more like watching a movie it is. Even if one of them cries out, stumbles, reaches up to pull heaven down, which they won't, there'll be a protective distance.

I've taken cover behind the hearse. A few feet away Ron Harvey's watching me. Maybe I'm sending out some kind of a message, and he's picked up on it. Maybe he knows I think I ought to be with them, the Gundersons, one of the principal mourners.

Aren't I more than just one of Dory's classmates? More than just one of the six suits rounded up to play a walk-on part? I don't even want to be with her family if they don't want me. But the feeling's there. I deserve it. I've got it coming to me.

Two of the funeral-home guys are suddenly among us, moving into action, doing what I was dreading all along. Somebody's opened the wide hearse door. We have to stand clear of it. The door falls back, and there's a watery flash of polished nickel. And inside, the end of the coffin, a burnished silver color.

It has no reality, and yet it's close enough to touch. I tell myself it's only a box, and yet it's either the head or the foot, so it's more than that.

It moves, grooved into a retractable framework of skids and ball bearings and toy wheels. A funeral director's hand guides it half out into the daylight before it begins to dip. He signals in the direction of Bill and Jay and the brother-in-law. They step up to one side. When Todd and Ron start past me to take the other side, I turn and we form up.

Between the two of them I see the rail that runs the length of the coffin. Todd's hand has already closed over it. Mine opens, fingers cramped. Touching it, being this near is another test I have to pass. There's this battery of tests, and I haven't even begun.

Then we have it in our hands, bearing the full weight. It distributes among us, though our shoulders bow in unison, three toward three. *Dead weight,*

13

I think, so somewhere down deep I must be out of control. *Don't let go.*

Then we're there, already sitting down, and whole minutes are missing. The six of us fill out the front row with Dory's family. And straight ahead of us, in the tent opening, the burnished silver coffin rests on a platform of thick tubing above a square of fake grass.

My mind goes for details. Todd Eames is on one side of me, and I see past the end of his pants leg the yellow blob of a construction boot. On my other side Ron Harvey's reaching up to unhitch the perfect knot of a silk rep tie from his Adam's apple. He shoots one snow-white cuff and then the other. He understands what to do with his blue-flanneled arms. Down the row from us Mrs. Gunderson's hands grip the top of her purse.

The man who walked her to the grave site stands up, becoming the minister. He opens a Bible. Gilt-edged pages flutter in the wind. I blank out what he reads. As the Bible closes over the bookmark, Miss Burman's arms open, hands coming up just to the level of her shoulders. Her fingers wiggle, drawing the eyes of the choir.

She nods, and they begin to sing. My stomach knots, but then relaxes when they move into an unfamiliar song, too soft, too thin at first. The melody and the first words are lost. This isn't the school music room, and they grasp this as Miss Burman takes a firmer hold on the outdoor space, throws her head back to remind them to project.

Their voices weave, and I resist the music until it tails off, a little ragged and underrehearsed.

14

A moment of silent prayer follows, while I pray for this to be over. Then right in the middle of the quiet I catch a glimpse of Dory. It's not significant, not even memorable.

She's banging her locker door shut and striding off down the hall, with that little skip in her walk. And she's talking over her shoulder to a friend—Carol MacIntosh, Linda Whitman, somebody. Just the way I've seen her a thousand times, with her dark hair caught to frame her face by one of the long-tailed scarves she winds around her neck.

The memory gets specific—only a few weeks ago. Under Dory's scarf and coat she's wearing a sweatshirt and tennis shorts. She's carrying her racket.

We're meeting after school to work on her backhand. Some tennis nut has cleared the school courts of snow, and we head out for some practice. I fall in beside her, and she swats at snowdrifts with her racket as we walk. Her bare knee parts her coat with every step, and I wallow in the contrast: the winter coat, the summer tennis outfit, sneakers in the snow. I feel last summer in her cold fingers clasped in mine.

Her backhand needs work. So does her serve. But I'm not her coach. I don't even play. I just keep sending the ball back across the frozen net, pretending I'm not cold. Pretending I know more about the game than I do.

The memory leaves me then, and I only remember I was colder on that court than I'd admit. When we were working on Dory's backhand.

The minister's speaking again, scanning the rows as he talks. Words I gladly let the wind take . . . her fine family . . . the fine young people gathered today to share their loss . . . the great, unquestionable mystery . . . and death as part of life, eternal life.

I hear too much, but keep it on the surface. I don't actually let it in.

It's quiet again, and people shift in their chairs. Behind the front row coughing is permissible. I wait for people to stir, stand up. But it isn't over. It may never be. Burman's arms are out, and her fingers are wiggling again. The choir's eyes are on her. At the first note I know this is more than I should have to handle. It's the song by Mendelssohn. This one's well rehearsed because they sang it at the winter concert. Meaning to go deaf, I go blind. First a blur, then some kind of rage. A soprano voice rises out of the rest and moves with a kind of unbearable certainty, every note clear in the air. I squint to see who it is.

Linda Whitman's mouth is moving, forming words. There's enough force and feeling in the way she's singing. But it's mechanical too, and she's working on her control. Burman probably volunteered her at the last minute. Linda's eyes look scared. And it's all wrong. Dory sang that solo part. It was hers. It's still hers.

Then it's over, and I'm one of the last to stand up. As pallbearers, we have nothing more to do. The coffin stays in full view, above an invisible pit. We're to leave it. This is no western movie where they lower a pine box into a hole while the mourners stand around on raw earth, leaning on shovels. Weirdly enough, this is real life.

"Okay?" Ron Harvey says, brushing by me. He's

the only one of the pallbearers who hasn't turned away.

"Yeah. Making it."

I don't know where to go. Beth and Dad and Gram are back there somewhere, cut off by the rows of chairs and the people beginning to fan out. They'd keep a low profile. That's their way.

I turn around, and Ruth-Ellen's suddenly in front of me. Dory's sister. She's about eleven, if that—fifth, sixth grade. I don't really relate to her, and this is no moment to start. But she's standing in front of me, away from her family. They've moved off, surrounded by their people.

Here's Ruth-Ellen. She's waiting for me to come to my senses, blocking my path to nowhere. Looking up at me with pink-rimmed, rabbit eyes in a face too pale.

"Mother says, would you come by the house, Matt?" There's this little sullen tug in her voice: grief-plus-being-eleven, I suppose. My mind's still not focusing.

She waits while I work out what she's said. She's about five feet tall, so I'm looking down at her forever. She plants a foot in the cemetery grass, reaches down, and rubs her knee.

She's wearing stockings—grown-up, flesh-colored type. She wants me to notice. This ridiculous message I seem to grasp.

"Your house?"

She nods. "Mother says—"

Her mother speaks through interpreters. She called our house yesterday and caught Beth just as she was

17

coming home from work. She asked Beth if I'd be a pallbearer. Now she's sent Ruth-Ellen to issue this . . . invitation. And Ruth-Ellen has obeyed. Ruth-Ellen who spends her days and nights plotting to overthrow her mother. But today, of course . . .

"Okay," I say. "I'll . . . drop by."

Her smudged eyes skate over to Ron Harvey and Bill Matlack. They're standing around, hands clasped behind their backs, unconsciously imitating the funeral directors.

But Ruth-Ellen's instructed to invite only me. She catches herself seeing past Ron and Bill to the coffin. Her head swivels, and she walks away fast with the little skip in her walk she's adopted.

The day keeps unfolding, lengthening: A Boston marathon complete with killer hills. Or is this the recognition I wanted? The family, the Gundersons including me in. One last time.

Chapter 3

The car knows the way. It noses out of the flat part of Glenburnie with all its right-angle streets, up the curving drive through the stone gates of Glenburnie Woods, the class part of town on the only real rise of land between here and the Chicago Loop. I've never been anyplace before knowing it was for the last time. And I'm remembering the first time.

Dory and I had been seeing a lot of each other around school before I picked her up at her house one night. I'd first run into her at school, of course. I ran into her hard. Those were the days when I was sprinting up stairs—any stairs—to strengthen my calf muscles. I hit her at my top speed on a landing. Nearly knocked her down. It was the only possible way I could meet a girl without chickening out.

And picking her up at her house was another landmark. We don't do much of that in Glenburnie, and they do less of it up in Glenburnie Woods. It's what her folks would call a date, which isn't a major term in our vocabulary. We're too cool for that kind of thing. Or we're trying to be.

I sat in the car out on the brick drive that night, wishing the house wasn't so big. There were gas-flame lanterns on both sides of the double front doors, and the ivy growing up three stories to the roof rustled like money. I must have figured that a girl like Dory would live in a house like this, but that didn't make ringing the doorbell any easier.

Dory let me in and gave my hand a squeeze. She led me to where her mother was sitting on a sofa at the end of an immense room. Over the mantel behind her was a painting of the three girls. Ruth-Ellen when she was small and round; Dory, the age Ruth-Ellen is now; and Jess, the older sister, looking grown-up already.

Her mother sat with one foot tucked up under her. "We've heard so much about you," she said, meaning she wouldn't mind hearing a little more.

And her dad loomed up, with a hand to shake. Dory wanted to get going, and so did I, but her mother said, "Darling, give your old mom and dad a break. We never see anything of you girls these days. Jess never calls, and Ruth-Ellen is continually upstairs behind a locked door. She seems to be spending her entire puberty in the bathroom."

"That's a lie," came Ruth-Ellen's voice from just outside the room somewhere.

Mr. Gunderson went to get us Cokes, and Dory shrugged and settled on the sofa, slipping a foot under herself, mirroring her mother. I wondered how close to her I should sit.

"Okay, Mother, we really want to get out of here before I'm supposed to be back home again, so let me condense for you."

I felt a little warm under the collar.

"Matt lives with his father and stepmother."

Mrs. Gunderson's eyebrow rose a centimeter.

Dory moaned a little. "Your mother—your own mother isn't living, is she, Matt?"

My throat was all dried out. "No. She hasn't been living for four years. I mean, she died four years ago. She was sick for a while, and then she . . . ah . . . died."

Mrs. Gunderson's mouth began to form a word: *where* . . .

But Dory went on. "They live in—what's it called, Matt?"

"Camelot Close."

Where? her mother's mouth began to form again.

I looked around for my tongue and found it. "It's an apartment complex, Mrs. Gunderson. On Beltline, out by the expressway."

Her eyes narrowed a little, trying to see that far. I figured she was visualizing it as sort of a rambling motel-type structure for renters. Which it sort of is.

I even volunteered some information, maybe to make a point. "My dad grew up around Glenburnie back when it was mainly a farm town. He went into the service when he was eighteen, did his twenty, and then came back here."

Mrs. Gunderson smiled, nodded encouragement.

"We had a house on Hawthorne when we first came back."

"But you moved into an apartment when you lost your mother," she said, still nodding.

"Not right then. We moved into the apartment when Dad married Beth—my stepmother. He thought maybe she wouldn't want to live in a house where—"

"Yes, of course," Mrs. Gunderson said, suddenly not wishing to pry.

We drank the Cokes down about halfway and got out. I'd decided we'd go to Gino's for a pizza, though we'd both had dinner and weren't particularly hungry. In fact it was about the first time in my life I hadn't been particularly hungry.

Bill Matlack and Alice Kirby were going to be at Gino's too. I'd set it up to have other people around in case the conversation got slow. Maybe I thought I might not be enough by myself.

But before we got to the car, I knew it was going to be fine. The dogwood shadows were all lacy on her face, and she looked up at me when she talked. She only came up to my upper arm, but then, I was ten feet tall that night. Taller, once we got away from her parents.

Today I can't park in their drive. Cars line both sides of the curving street for the whole last block.

When I get up to the double doors, they open before I can ring the bell. It's Jess, the married sister. "You're Matt, aren't you?" She holds on to the door even after it's open. "I'm glad you came. Mother . . ."

She can't deal with me on a one-to-one basis. I find my way through the empty hall and down the step into the big living room. It's full of people and low voices and the drifting smell of coffee.

Ruth-Ellen's moving around the room, weaving among the big people. Her face is pinched up, but she's jittery with some kind of excitement. Women sitting on the sofas put their hands out to draw her in, pat her, calm her down. Their hands slide down her arm, and she keeps weaving.

A woman I don't know comes up and says, "I expect you'd like some coffee."

She leads me out to the sunporch, where the coffee urn's set up on a garden table. A group of women who look like they all belong to the same club are setting out the cups and plates of cookies.

One of them's saying, "I don't know how she's going to be able to cope with this. The suddenness . . ."

They see me and stop talking. One lady makes a big business of filling a cup. The others point out the cookies. Eat, their smiles say. You're young. You won't suffer like the grownups. Bring your friends.

I'm this minority in the sunporch though, so their eyes slide past me to the door, hoping there'll be others.

"Oh, Jess," one of them says. She's standing, teetering in her high heels on the threshold. Her arms are folded with hands cupping her elbows.

"Matt? Would you? Mother . . ."

She leads me back across the living room to the little den at the back of the house. "Mother, it's Matt," she says at the door. I make myself walk past her into the den.

Mrs. Gunderson's standing at the window. Her fingers are splayed out on the pane, and her forehead's resting against the back of her hand. She turns around, reacting too slow to Jess.

"Oh, yes." She touches a table for balance. "Come in."

But I'm already in. Her mouth looks blurred. "I was just saying to Dory the other day . . ."

She starts again. "They tell me she died of something called a berry aneurysm. Isn't that a strange name for anything?"

I look at the floor. I don't know where else to look. I don't know how Dory died, not exactly. All I know is what I heard afterward. That between fifth and sixth period she walked out of school. Nobody remembered seeing her go. She went out into the parking lot and fell between two parked cars.

She must have felt sick or dizzy. Maybe she went out for some air. I don't even know who found her. I must have been down in the locker room changing when the ambulance came. I didn't know anything until after school, when I swung past her locker. There were already rumors, nobody being too sure about anything. Some people being a little too excited, getting off on any minor mystery.

"A berry aneurysm," Mrs. Gunderson says again, reciting, chanting what the doctors have told her. "It's a blockage of the arteries feeding the brain. And when it happens very near the brain, it destroys the centers for circulation. It stopped her breathing."

I don't know how much of this I can take, but I suppose Mrs. Gunderson has to get it said. I can see

24

she's stoned—on Librium or Valium or whatever they've given her.

"We couldn't have foreseen it," she says. "We couldn't have known or done anything. And neither could you."

I shake my head, still staring down. I've wondered if there was something I should have noticed.

"You're not responsible," she says. And then: "I was just saying to Dory the other day, 'You know you really ought to see more boys. Different boys.'"

She looks at something just past my shoulder and goes on. "Nothing against you necessarily. But what I meant was that Dory should—keep her options open. She's so young. But you know Dory. She's so emphatic in her opinions—like me."

She's not going to remember anything she's saying, even though she means every word. I try to think about something else to blot her out, but there isn't anything else.

"I think you should put all this behind you," she says. "I don't think it would have worked out between you and Dory anyway. So many differences."

"I better go, Mrs. Gunderson."

"Yes." She starts to turn back to the window. "You run along now. You'll find someone else. It won't take you long."

I get out of there, wanting to make a run through the living room, but Jess is there, waiting. She catches my arm. "Was she able to talk? I'm so afraid—"

"She talked," I say. Then I slip out of her grip and make it to the front door, and through it. Then I'm in the car, somewhat safe. I've forgotten where the ignition is, and I'm trying to bend the wheel around the steering column. But then I ease off, and I'm just sitting in this empty car.

I don't think it would have worked out between you and Dory, Mrs. Gunderson's voice says again. She speaks from the empty seat beside me, where Dory sat.

"I never even saw her," I say out loud, maybe to Mrs. Gunderson. I never saw her lying in the parking lot. But I can see her there now. Very still, with a pebble or two of parking lot gravel in her hand.

But I never saw her today, not in that silver box. And when I walked out of the cemetery, I wasn't really walking away from her. Or toward anything.

It seems reasonably clear to me, sitting here in the tomb of the car. Dory's alive. I'm dead.

Chapter 4

Little kids are still playing in the long evening, hunkered together up on the jungle gym, when I pull into the parking lot. All around the apartment complex the kitchens are lit up.

In ours something's in the microwave oven, and the table's set. In the living room the TV's giving tomorrow's weather. I cross the hall to my room, pulling my tie off. It's five fifteen by my clock radio, plenty of time to change and get to work, since I don't feel like supper.

I'm sitting on the bed picking at a shoelace when the door moves. Knuckles brush the far side of it. Dad. He's never knocked first in his life. He shuffles his feet, still invisible.

The door edges open, and he's there, out of his funeral clothes except for the white shirt. His baggy corduroys almost cover up the old army touch: spit-shined regulation black shoes.

27

"Matt? Dinner in about ten minutes, Beth says."

"I'll pass it up," I say. "I'll go straight to work."

He brushes away something in the air with a square hand. "Don't worry about that. Cal called and said don't bother coming in tonight. Ron's working, and between them they can handle it. Says it's not worth staying open Thursday nights anyway."

"But he will," I say. "Everything in the mall stays open till nine Thursdays. It's in their contract."

Dad runs a hand around the back of his neck. "Why don't you just knock off tonight and—take it easy."

"I'd sooner be working, Dad."

He's not going to question this, but he hangs in there. "Did you stop by the Gundersons' this afternoon, afterwards?"

I nod, and he says, "They're pretty cut up, I guess."

I look up at him. The ceiling light has found all the gray in his hair. I want to challenge him about what he's just said. But I don't know why, so I don't know how.

I leave then, slipping out fast, past Beth's dinner.

From the expressway I see the only cars in the mall parking lot are down by the Jewel, where they hold the Saturday flea market. I park right in front of Cal's Collegiate Corner, which appears to be customerless. Cal's behind the front counter pinning a tattersall shirt onto a headless dummy. It's ten to six. I could rotate the tires and still be early.

To keep the Collegiate Corner halfway viable, Cal's tried to touch all the bases: Brooks Brothers type haberdashery for the commuter, tapered work shirts, a meager rack of rentable tuxes for prom night, Jordache jeans. And the Jogger's Jungle, an afterthought piled with Adidas running shoes, sweat shirts, sweatbands in rainbow colors, jogging shorts with waistbands up to forty-two inches.

I lock the car and collapse the antenna to discourage vandals. Cal spits pins at my entrance, hoping for a customer. "Hey, Matt, you didn't have—"

"I know."

"I called your dad to tell—"

"I know."

He pulls a loose thread from the shirt. "Listen, I'm sorry—"

"I know that too, Cal."

We're spared more of this because Ron Harvey walks in behind me, early as usual. This part-time job is major with him. In nearly two years of work he hasn't drawn a penny in real salary. He takes his entire pay in merchandise at an employee's discount.

He's changed into what must be the season's big look. Layer on preppie layer. A cotton turtleneck under a Lacoste shirt with turned-up collar under a red Pendleton wool shirt under a wet-look fingertip jacket with laid-back drawstring hood. Unbleached jeans, cuffed, over Eddie Bauer chukkas. A walking, top-of-the-line ad for the Collegiate Corner.

Ron's a born salesman, but the stockroom's my beat. I'm only called out front to sell a sweatsuit to a weight-watcher or to fit a pair of Puma running shoes.

Ron only nods toward me. He knows what kind of a day it's been.

29

I work till closing time, ticketing packages of three-for-the-price-of-two boxer shorts. The only oddity of the evening is how ordinary it is. And how my hands conduct business as usual.

At nine Ron comes back to the stockroom and eases himself up onto the wrapping table. He fingers a Kent Light out from around a tape measure in his Pendleton pocket, lights up, blows smoke away from me.

Because I've been spotted running the track sixth period, he sees me as some kind of Bruce Jenner inhaling with spotless pink lungs. But I'm not a team player, not even a second-string anything. He's never been able to quite peg me. Still, he cups his Kent Light and tries to control the smoke.

"A hundred and fifty and change," he says, summing up his slow-night sales. Then, with a wicked smile: "Cal came in at seventy-nine ninety-five—that goosedown pile jacket from the winter sale rack."

He'll never interest me in the clothing business. Still, it's a safe enough topic tonight. "A little over two hundred and thirty," I compute, "which means he ought to be able to make the payroll."

"Man, you're a miserable, miserly packrat." Ron thumps his chukkas together and casts his eyes across the smoky ceiling. "You know?"

I do. With money, I'm squirrely in the extreme. I'll save practically every dime they don't deduct. I've got car insurance to pay on, and I like some time off in the summer up at the lake.

My priorities and Ron's fit like a threaded pipe. If I was up front in a twenty-button blazer trying to outsell him, he'd be ducking out on coffee breaks to slash my tires, tie my antenna in bowknots. I've told him this. He agrees.

These are about the boundaries of our friendship. Except right now when he's talking like it's any normal night. This may be what I need. Or maybe not.

I'm home by ten, which is early for Dad to be in bed. But he must be, because Beth's sitting at the kitchen table, smoking. And she only smokes when he's not around: a very light-tar, low-nicotine, long-filter brand. The exhaust fan's on, and she blows smoke toward it. We live in an age of anxious vices.

She's in her bathrobe, waiting to feed me now, and I'm going to let her. "There's lasagna," she says. "Maybe a little dry, but hot. I couldn't keep the salad fresh, but there's applesauce. It's Lola's home-canned."

I pull a chair up to the table, and she slides a heaping plate in front of me. She must know I don't want anything to eat. But I'm a big boy now, and I don't reject her offerings. We've been pretty careful with each other in the almost two years she's been my stepmother. She isn't completely sure I don't resent her. I haven't been able to tell her I'm not sure what we'd do without her. This could even be the night, except the subject's emotional, and the day's been long.

I wave a forkful of lasagna at her, signaling how good it probably tastes.

"I bet it's dried out," she says, lighting up another

cigarette. She's washed all the makeup off her face, improving herself. She borders on beautiful and doesn't even know it. I've never tried anything as bold as telling her. I don't even give her a Valentine. They probably don't make them for stepmothers.

"You know," she says in a careful voice, "I never really knew Dory."

They met on that weekend up at the cottage last summer. The Gundersons let Dory go up there only that one time. They may have thought a stepmother didn't fill the bill as a chaperone. They may have thought a lot of things. I've spent quite some time wondering about what the Gundersons thought.

"Shall I not say anything more?" Beth says.

"No. Talk. Nobody's talked to me all day. All I've heard are words."

She thinks about that and doesn't seem to find it crazy talk. "I did like her," she says. "I mean I don't know if we'd have had anything in common. She was like the girls I sort of knew when I was in high school. The ones in the college-prep classes. I was in secretarial and business English, but they were always, you know—"

"The stars," I say.

She searches my face. "Well, yes. They all seemed to have plans, and all I had were dreams."

I've never heard Beth talk like this before. I wish I knew how to tell her what she's just said is great.

But I can't, so I say, "There were probably a lot of people who thought I was really pushing it, going after Dory. You know, batting a little above my league."

She stubs out an unfinished weed and turns her

hand over on the table, dismissing these people and what they think. "They had it a little wrong, didn't they?"

"Did they?"

"I think so. You didn't go after Dory. She always made her own decisions, didn't she?"

"And a few of mine," I say, almost smiling. "Maybe you're right. It's pretty much what her mother said to me today. She said Dory was like her."

"Was she?"

"No. Yes."

Suddenly I feel sullen, kidlike. Where's all the grief, the mature, adult-style despair that's been dogging me all day? I'm pouting because Dory's mother, stoned and stunned and destroyed, said a few wrong things to me.

"Why in the hell," I say to Beth, "do women think they're the only ones who can feel anything?"

"Do we?"

"All day long people have been worried out of their skulls about how Mrs. Gunderson's going to survive. I lost Dory too."

"I know."

"She didn't."

"You're making allowances for the fact that she's in shock, aren't you?" Beth says.

"Yes, I am, which is more than she was willing to do for me."

Beth's looking down at the tablecloth. "I don't know," she says. "I'm not anybody's mother. I never have quite figured out who I am. I don't know if we women think we've got a corner on emotions. All I know is, your dad went to bed early tonight because he didn't know what to say to you. And I sat up waiting for you, but I didn't know what to say either."

The room wobbles in front of my eyes. "I . . . appreciate it, Beth."

"I wish I could do something for you, Matt."

"You have."

"Oh, no." She turns her hand over again, dismissing herself this time. "But somebody will."

I didn't believe her. I didn't even know what she meant.

Chapter 5

It's slated to be a too-typical day. The black choir robes are going to be back in the closet, and there won't even be a moment of silent prayer for Dory over the P.A. system. We don't pray in school. It's illegal, and even if it wasn't, we're all too equal for that. All the little gods and goddesses are milling around outside school, swapping gossip and controlled substances before the first bell. I'm working on a really foul mood that may get me through the day.

But first I have to find a parking space. The vast, somewhat rippled hood of the El Camino wanders up and down the jammed rows. In one of these rows, between two of these cars—

I rein in my mind by figuring how much of my life I've spent cruising parking lots for an empty space. Our parents carpool, resort to bikes, stand frozen at bus stops. But my generation flows through the world on the last of the fossil fuels. And not even the nonreaders have ever flunked the driving test.

I park in a plowed field three blocks away. The school squats on the horizon. Walking back, I kill time by matching cars with drivers. Everybody's here already, and still I'm not late. Time has slowed down recently, and it's impossible not to be early.

I have no trouble identifying the silver Porsche 924 Turbo, parked at an angle with its incredible snout blocking half a parking place reserved for faculty. It belongs to Royce Eburt, stud senior. In half an hour a P.A. announcement will flood the school, requesting him to move it, which should be good for a laugh in the locker room. The day is already predictable, prepackaged.

Bill Matlack's tooling along the crowded concrete in front of the main doors astride his Honda 450, herding the pedestrians. Right and left hands rest over throttle and clutch. He's moving slow, and his boot's already drifting back to the kickstand.

Creeping opposite, also parade-slow, Sheri Martinson is piloting her midnight-blue Celica Supra with Royce Eburt riding shotgun. The king and queen of the seniors are conducting their morning motorcade.

If anybody remembers yesterday, they seem to have themselves pretty well under control. I cross the parade route where Alice Kirby's standing, waiting for Bill Matlack to part with his Honda.

She sees me, and her face drops into a sad mask. "Oh, Matt, listen, I'm really wrecked about—"

But Bill's swerved the Honda up beside us. It slips sideways under his crotch, and he throws out a steadying boot. "Smokin' and strokin'," he says loud in my ear, looking past me at Alice. He guns the Honda in neutral, blatting out all human sound. Alice lifts her shoulders, and we're all off the hook. The bell seems to have rung during the Honda sound. I go with the flow.

First period is Contemporary Social Issues, the school's favorite elective. Class enrollment may run to sixty, but there's never more than fifteen at once. The teacher, Bob Katz—Bobcat behind his back and sometimes to his face—is a casual roll-taker. And if you're not marked absent first period, you're not absent all day long.

I haven't figured out any other advantage to the class. I should have taken American History and broken my tail doing some real work. Dory did.

Bobcat's sitting on his desk in his shirtsleeves. Behind him is a detailed map of the Middle East with Saudi Arabia big and defenseless and Russia looking down on it from above. Bobcat pulls at his mustache and draws his ankles up into the lotus position. We approach contemporary social issues on a personal note, our usual way.

"So," he's saying to his faithful followers in the front circle, "where are your heads today, problem-wise?" He talks in the language of his lost youth, but we manage to follow him. It's the only class requirement.

Denise Mills has her chair tipped back at an astounding angle. She's searching the ceiling, looking for a contemporary social issue. Her chair clumps down onto four feet. Denise is about to contribute. She's got a plastic barrette parked up by the part in her hair. She pries it out and begins to fiddle with it. "You know," she says, "a really main drain on me personally, and I'm sure everybody else feels it too . . ."

She looks around the room, checking on who's dropped in.

"Right on, Denise," Bobcat says above her, "go with that."

"Well, what really gets me down, and I'm like really feeling it right now, you know? A really major pain with me these days is the seniors."

People behind the first circle moan, slump, open Algebra 2 books, search bags for ball-points to finish English assignments.

In a caring voice Bobcat asks, "What makes you think the seniors are on your case, Denise?"

"My what? Oh. You know how they are. Like they've just all heard back from their colleges. I mean, they all know where they're going now, and they could care less about anything else, you know?"

"So what, Denise?" says somebody from behind me.

She seems not to hear. "I'm sick of this really stupid senior attitude." Her fist drops onto her notebook, completely graffitied with the names of senior boys.

Bobcat runs both hands through his wild hair, smoothing it back over the bald spot. "How does this make you feel, Denise?"

Somebody gives out an audible groan, and Denise tells us how it makes her feel, in four letters.

A hissing giggle comes from in front of me, from

38

Le Vien Dieu. His skinny bottom takes up only half the seat, and his miniature khaki shirt sighs with starch. An extra ball-point is wedged over his ear. He's making notes like crazy, working up his vocabulary. But Denise's four letters have broken his rhythm.

He's from Vietnam, one of the Boat People who escaped and made their way in stages to the other side of the world: Glenburnie. He's in this class because his English isn't good enough yet for anything heavier. Neither is Denise's, but that's a different case. In Le Vien Dieu we have an authentic Contemporary Social Issue, but Bobcat has never called on him. Instead, he's asking Denise to make closer contact with her gut reactions.

"How do you think you'll handle it this time next year when you're a senior, Denise?"

"She'll never make it," somebody says. But she will. Everybody will. She tosses her head around, jamming the barrette back in her hair, and throws a leg up on her desk. On her foot is an incredible shoe: a free-form cork sculpture with straps embedded in her ankle.

"I don't want to talk about it anymore," Denise says. Her red and black fingernail traces a name on her notebook.

My attention, such as it is, flips from the Middle East map to Bobcat, from Denise's shoe to the glossy back of Le Vien Dieu's head. But I've played with these ironies before. And will again. Denise and Le Vien Dieu are the only two people who never cut this class.

I'm not even particularly annoyed with Denise, and annoyance is the best she's ever gotten out of anybody. Today I even understand her, know where she's coming from, as Bobcat would put it. She needs the seniors because when she looks around closer to her life, there's nobody there. I begin to know the feeling.

The rest of the morning is this meaningless and about this absurd. During free period I walk down the road, avoiding the parking lot, and sit in the car until I see I'm trying to bend the wheel around the steering column again.

Third period is English Literature—BritLit. We're doing poetry or something. Mrs. Tolliver hands out Xerox sheets, talks about an assignment, but I fail to hear the deadline for it.

By lunch I'm only about 10 percent there. Eyes straight ahead, I walk right through two of the other ex-pallbearers, Todd Eames and Jay Rosen. They're both Glenburnie Woods types, more Dory's people than mine, if I have any. They move apart, and I plow through.

And down the stairs to the lower hall, heading for Dory's locker before I realize I'm going there to meet her as usual.

Her locker door's open, and people are standing around it. Dory's always surrounded by people. I see Linda Whitman's back, screening the others. Linda, with a dancer's long spine and a singer's voice, always poised, posed, like a performer waiting in the wings.

And where Linda Whitman is, Carol MacIntosh

can't be far away. Linda bends down, looking into the back of Dory's locker, and there's Carol standing beside the opening. I almost don't know her because she isn't laughing or talking or doing anything.

Linda and Carol and Dory, the inseparables since kindergarten. The inventors of the sleep-over. The undiscovered outlaws who wrapped every house in Glenburnie Woods in toilet paper as late as ninth-grade Halloween and were even then too cool, too mature, too—untouchable to be accused. The inseparables.

There's somebody else there, down on her knees in front of the locker. Time spins back, and it's last week again.

She edges back and stands up. It's Dory's sister—Jess. The logic of it slams me in the face. Jess has come to school to clean out Dory's locker. She stands up, burdened with books and one of Dory's long-tailed scarves.

They stand there a minute, the three of them. And I keep my distance while people push past me at the bottom of the stairs. Then Carol puts her hand over her mouth, and her eyes dissolve. Linda's head bows. I see the curve of her neck through her hair. And Jess says something to them. Maybe she realizes she's the only adult, and somebody has to be in control. Yet they've had to lead her to the locker because they're the only ones who'd know Dory's combination. Except me.

In the cafeteria I drink a carton of milk at a table full of tenth-graders.

Then Algebra 2 and then Chemistry and then the

41

break between fifth and sixth period when in this same week Dory walked out of school and died on me.

Sixth period. The tag end of the day, P. E. If you're a hard-core jock, you have varsity sports. If you're tennis team, you get in your car and drive four blocks to the courts. If you're water polo or swim team, you report to the pool. If you're an organized runner, you report to either the indoor or the outdoor coach.

And if you're not into any of this, you've negotiated an independent contract with the coach-of-your-choice. You can do your running or put your shot or even hit a tub full of golf balls for an hour on your own for course credit.

When I finally got through to the outdoor coach that I wasn't about to jog in a pack, I got my lonely runner contract and can walk straight out of school and drive home if I feel like it.

But today I decide to run, possibly in the forest preserve. I may need to do some stretches first. I haven't run for several years now—since yesterday morning at the lake.

I get there late to have the locker room to myself. And I'm sitting in front of my locker in a jock strap and a T-shirt, pulling on sweat socks, when suddenly I get company.

Joe Hoenig looms up at the end of the locker aisle. Off the field Joe's slow. But he has nothing to be in a hurry about, since an injury benched him last November in his senior season in the game against Glenbrook North. I guess I know him. Everybody knows a first-string quarterback famed for his quick release.

"How's it going?" he rumbles.

I decide against telling him, but manage a friendly enough shrug.

He drops his pants. "Damn knee," he says, peering down at himself. His knee joint was famous last fall, even making the *Chicago Tribune* when it took one lateral lick too many. He's bunching upper-leg muscles with his creature hand so he can see down past his thigh. He peers and squints and considers. He may even be inviting me to have a look.

"Sucker's still swollen," he mutters at this knee. It may be. It's huge. But then, so's the other one. "There's no doubt about it. This has cost me the Heisman Trophy."

His attention shifts from his knee to me, a penetrating ice-blue gaze.

Jocks take themselves so much to heart that I miss the point. But somehow I realize this is a joke. Joe doesn't actually see himself as a future Heisman hopeful, not even a failed one. I start to shrug, but I've already done that, so I grin.

He flops down on the bench, which gives under him like a trampoline. Then he bounces, scooting off his underpants. I'm digging around in the bottom of my locker for my running shorts. He's naked and winding himself in a towel the size of a nine-by-twelve rug. And he's just standing there, leaning against the locker bank.

"Whirlpool for me," he says. "I've spent this whole stinking winter in that whirlpool. Man, I have been

Jacuzzied. Feel like a stewed prune. Doesn't do squat for the knee, of course. And I'm about to shrivel up totally."

"You got a long way to go before that happens, man," I say.

He smiles, scratches his bushy mane, shifts his towel. Then he comes out with a surprise. "You're Moran, aren't you?"

You never think a jock will know you back.

"You and Dory Gunderson were an item." It's not even a question. I nod again and wad up my regular clothes to aim them into the depths of the locker.

"You don't want to talk about it probably," Joe says.

What is this guy to me? "I don't know what to say about it. I still don't even believe it."

He sits back down on the bench, and his doorknob toes peer out from under the towel. I guess we're going to have a conversation.

"I had this girl once," he says. "She went to Maine Township. I thought it was great having a girl who went to another school. You could have this relationship without being distracted all the time. That's where my head was then, when I thought anything else had to come in second to football. Game plan first, life second, you know?"

He points to his famous knee. "That's all over now, of course."

I sit there, completely suited up, wondering what my role in this discussion's supposed to be. I don't seem to recognize friendliness when it's staring me in the face. "What happened? With the girl, I mean."

Joe sweeps his locker door shut with a casual,

pile-driver hand. "You can picture it. S⌄ started up with some guy at Maine Township. W⌄ else?"

"So what did you do?"

"Well, first I creamed Glenbrook South. Then I creamed Deerfield. Then I creamed Niles West. Then I creamed Niles North."

He recites the roster of our football opponents up till that November game when his knee made news. I visualize heaps of dismembered limbs on fifty-yard lines all over the northern suburbs. And bodies in numbered jerseys hanging from goalposts, turning in the wind. He's still talking.

"You know what I do now? I get in the old Toyota Fastback and drive over to Maine Township around the time they're getting out of school. And I just sit there across the street, figuring maybe I'll see her coming out. I never actually have. I don't know what I'd do if I did. Probably nothing. I just go over there sometimes."

Can I picture Joe Hoenig shoe-horned into a Toyota, sitting out in front of some other school, waiting for a girl he's not going to be able to talk to? Somehow I can.

"It's different, though, with you," he's saying. "I'm not comparing the situations."

And he isn't. Is he trying—I don't even know the word for it. Is he trying to comfort me?

"Dory Gunderson was dynamite," he says. "I always noticed her. Had plenty of time to this winter. What else was there to do? These girls who've really got it all together. I like that. Even the way they move."

I'm having trouble following what he's saying.

45

He's being as subtle as he knows how to be, maybe too subtle for me.

"Come off it, Joe," I say. "There are plenty of girls for the"—I almost say *hotshot*—"first-string team."

He snorts, rubs his nose. "Gridiron groupies. Their offense is great. My defense is better."

"Meaning?" Joe begins to interest me. I didn't know team players had inner lives.

"I've got this Incredible Hulk image, and the people I want to take me seriously don't."

"Girl people," I say.

"Like that," he says. "You're a runner."

"No. I just run."

"I kind of envy that," he says. "You can handle being out there on your own."

"I'm finding out I can't."

This quiets Joe for a minute. His arms are folded against his chest. Enormous biceps. Big, pointy teardrop elbows. Forearms like fur-bearing steel. Knuckles like machine parts.

He looks up at the wire grill on the overhead light, possibly getting ready to go off on another tangent. "You know that game we had with Evanston? It was Homecoming, and the coach got us overpsyched. We were in here at halftime without a point to our name, and guys were praying, screaming for blood, going very ape. And the coach was working up a coronary on his own. Man, it was a scene. Then in the second half all we got was a five-yard penalty for delaying the game while we tried to get our act together, which we never did. And that was one of the better moments. Wipe-out. Total wipe-out."

Joe sighs at this instant replay.

"And we weaseled in here afterwards and didn't know what to do with ourselves. We didn't even shower. Albertson took a swing at Kovac just to relieve his tension, and hit the wall instead.

"Then I look over here, right here on this bench, about where you are. And I see Crock Wilson. You know Crock. Six-foot-five and weighs about an eighth of a ton. I mean he can rattle your cage.

"And Crock's just slumped over there with his elbows on his knees and his hands hanging down. Just sitting there in his hip pads with his wrists taped up like a mummy. And he's crying. He's crying his dumb heart out. There's a puddle on the floor. Right where you're sitting."

Joe's come to the end of his story, and I don't know what to make of it.

"What I'm saying, man, is: You've got some crying to do. Just do it."

And then Joe Hoenig limps off to the whirlpool.

Chapter 6

Crying's out. You can break down, but does it bring anybody back? It doesn't make sense. Nothing much does until I get the first of my great ideas.

It takes a few days, but school in its pointless way helps. I get about a bellyful of listening to Bobcat give Denise therapy. I have it up to here with Mrs. Tolliver's Xerox sheets in BritLit. I've sat long enough in the cafeteria watching Linda Whitman and Carol MacIntosh restructure their friendship as a twosome, with the guys from their group around them again and beginning to swarm.

I hit on this great solution. You get drunk— seriously wasted. Maybe you stay that way.

There are certain complications. I'm old enough to feel considerable pain, but not old enough to buy the cure over the counter. This is where Ron Harvey comes in. He's a senior, and seniors have their uses. He's just observed his eighteenth birthday. I invite him to celebrate it by buying me a couple of six packs and a quart of Scotch. That should do it.

In this conversation we have in Cal's stockroom Ron big-brothers me, tries to talk me out of it. I've mentioned this straight-arrow image I have in his eyes. But then, he's fairly fascinated at how quick I start peeling five-dollar bills out of my back pocket, considering what a miserable, miserly packrat I am about money.

He fills my order at the mall liquor store on his coffee break, and it's in a brown bag beside me in the car after work. I don't invite Ron along. This is not a party.

I drive around nighttime streets, looking for the right place, the proper setting. Glenburnie is not the proper setting. What we need here is a little distance.

Somehow I'm on Golf Road heading east, half burned out on my plans alone. Fairly pleased with myself at how well this project is going to work out. Simple solutions are often the best. I pat the brown bag beside me. *87-20*

The car penetrates alien territory. Towns merge with each other around country clubs. I'll drive as far as I can go in this direction and find the perfect place. I'll hit the Lake Michigan shoreline after the T-intersection with Sheridan Road, and there'll be this nice quiet beach.

I brake for the Green Bay Road cross traffic. Past it over the Chicago & Northwestern tracks is the big-money area: Winnetka, Wilmette, somewhere. And then Sheridan Road. But it's dark, disorienting. There are a lot of mansions and walls between me and my destination.

Heading south, I find the perfect spot. Among the mansions there's a little park with the beach beyond. Even a lighthouse. This must be the place.

Killing the lights, I take my pick of parking places. Nobody's around. The night's cold, but I'll soon be feeling warm—cozy, rosy. The brown bag on the seat beside me is opening itself. Help is on the way.

Across the dark park the beach is even better, down a dip and safe from prying eyes. I stalk along a crust of sand, bearing my precious brown bag, looking for a place out of the wind.

Lake Michigan is nothing like little Juniper, where you can see the opposite shoreline. This is the big time. I find my place out of the wind. An old bench on its side almost under the dead-eyed lighthouse. Far to the south, Chicago curves twinkling out into the lake through an amber haze. I settle on the sand with my back against the bench, and pop the top on the first beer.

I'm not wild about beer, but this isn't the point. Sipping will take me all night. I try chugalugging and gag.

I've got to make this work, since nothing else has. I take long, deep drafts and breathe in between, observing the level line of the lake over the curve of the can. The lake is a shade blacker than the sky, except for the luminous foam on the waves hitting the beach. The only sounds there are for maybe an hour are the waves and the pop of my pop-top cans.

After the first three beers I am the lake: fathoms deep and beginning to lap the shore. To increase my capacity I'm drinking on an empty stomach. Full now, I'm only sleepy, so I practice drinking with shut eyes. I invite my mind to wander, but it only wanders to my bladder. I need to stand up, but I'm carrying this barrel of beer in me. So I roll on my side and unzip my pants.

This is ridiculous. This is the kind of thing you try only if you're drunk. And I'm not even near. I'm cold sober, and cold. After the fourth or fifth beer, I remember the Scotch.

Its lid doesn't pop, and I wonder about this. It's a screw-top surrounded by a waxy sealer. Trust Ron Harvey to pick the best brand my money can buy. I fumble it, sliver a thumbnail, unscrew the lid.

I'll be needing the full quart, so I decide to throw the lid into the lake. But in this prone position, my aim's off. The lid skips down the beach, or maybe behind the bench.

The Scotch has a nice cutting edge to chase the beer. It burns all the way down, searing fuzz out of my throat, and causing quite a bit of excitement in my stomach. I hold the bottle up to the horizon to see how much I've drunk, but my hand covers what the label doesn't. I'm lying flat now, my head clear of the bench, but I've made a little holder-hole in the sand for the Scotch bottle. I arch my arm around so's not to elbow it over. I marvel at how sober I still am.

And then there's this figure walking up the beach toward me, an outline against the distant lights of Chicago. She comes nearer. It's Dory, and I am so damn glad to see her.

She moves along the beach, darker than the dark except there's the white glow of the waves in her outline. I reach out to her, but I don't want to knock over the Scotch bottle. And she doesn't hear me when I yell. Even when I cut loose and scream.

She just walks by between me and the lake. I can see some of her plain as day, but not all of her. Parts are missing, and yet I know she's perfect—and really there. She's here and I'm here, and it's night down by the lake, so it must be last summer, so what could be wrong?

But she won't turn my way. She hasn't been letting me see her face lately. Maybe I've hurt her feelings or something. Basically I'm somewhat crude, but I think she'll forgive me if I can just scream loud enough.

The wind's whipping the long-tailed scarf around her neck, but still she won't look at me. She's moving on up the beach, without the skip in her walk, away from me. And boy, am I crying now.

Hands hand me around, lean me against cold metal—a car door. Something on the top of the car is revolving blue and white light square in my face. And somebody has a hand in my hip pocket. I know everything that's going on, of course. The blue and white light means cop car. So there'll be a crippled deer by the road somewhere back in the dark.

"I.D.," somebody says. "A driver's license if we get lucky."

This too is clear. "In my car," I say, every word separately shaped. "Over the visor."

"What's he trying to say?" says the voice.

"Are you the El Camino?" says another voice, right beside me. A voice possibly related to the hand that's holding me up by the back of my jacket collar.

"The El Camino is mine," I explain. "A sixty-five, the best year of the breed. Notice the chrome."

"Try the El Camino," says a voice. "It's the only vehicle in the vicinity."

There's the wheeze of leather jackets behind me and a lot of small talk. I see nothing but blue and white lights, alternating.

After a time a voice again: "Matt Moran. Age seventeen. Let's match you up with your picture." I'm turned around, completely blind from the lights. But I am so sober that I know they're comparing me with the photograph on my driver's license. This should just about clear up any lingering doubts in anybody's mind.

"Well, Matt, old buddy," the voice says, "we're going to have to take you downtown. You're not feeling sick, are you?"

"I enjoy top-notch health," I point out. "My attendance is fair to good, and you can verify this with the school records."

"Cat's got his tongue," says a voice. "Let's take him in. I'm freezing my tail."

And pretty soon I'm sitting in the set for *Barney Miller*. There's even coffee, and I can have all I want. It's warm in here, and I'm feeling cozy-rosy with all this steam heat and all these blue shirts and all these typewriters clacking away.

An officer of the law is sitting in a chair facing mine. He wants to be my friend.

"Now here's the way it is, Matt. If we can get hold of your folks, maybe we won't have to book you. You weren't drinking in your car, were you?"

"Drinking and driving don't mix," I remind him.

"What? Oh. Right. You got a dad, Matt?"

I nod, and he understands this completely. I'm beginning to get across to these people. "My dad's in quality control at a plant in the Industrial Park."

"He work the night shift?"

"No," I say. "Days."

"It's night now, Matt. What's his phone number at home?"

It's on the tip of my tongue.

"See if there's a Moran in the Glenburnie directory," someone says.

Since it's night, I'm pretty tired. I sleep awhile in the chair and rest my head on a handy desk blotter. Time passes, but my friend wants to talk some more.

"You were down on the beach by yourself, weren't you, Matt?"

I raise my head, shake it. "No. I wasn't alone. Dory was there."

"He was alone," Dad says.

Dad's here. He puts a hand on my shoulder and then gets behind me to lift me up by the armpits. I'm taller than he is, but he's stronger. I'm standing there in the crook of his arm with all these other people watching me. I'm the center of attention, so I probably ought to say something.

"A boy needs his dad," I tell the whole group of them. Then something completely unexpected happens. It could happen to anybody, and now it happens to me. Scotch-flavored beer appears briefly in my throat. Then I throw up. Right on an officer of the law. He jumps back, but I catch him from the knees down. I wouldn't have had a thing like that happen for the world.

Chapter 7

I wake up in my own bed, a little surprised. A lot seems to have happened, but I can't exactly put my finger on it. The slant of the sun says it's morning, and I think my clock radio reads ten till eight. Through the paper-thin walls I hear voices out in the kitchen.

Is this a school day or not? The muffled voices through the wall become Dad's, Beth's, and Gram's. Gram sometimes stops by on her way to work, and since this is the way my luck's running, she's picked today.

After a while—time means nothing—the door opens wide, and Gram's standing there. Her supermarket uniform is wrapped around her, and there's a handkerchief with purple threads pinned under her LOLA employee's nametag. Her hands are on her hips.

"He don't look sick to me." She comes nearer on crepey soles. I'm not wearing a T-shirt or a pajama top. I'm not sure if I'm wearing anything, so I pull the sheet up to my chin. She glances at the ceiling. "Heavens above, I've seen all of you there is, boy. They tell me you're sick, but you don't look it."

Then she's bending over the bed, only a little because she's short. Her long, jangling earrings swing free, and her nose twitches—a rabbity twitch.

She stands back and gives me a glinty, bifocal look. "For Pete's sake, you smell like a brewery. They said you were sick and had me worried. You're *drunk*."

"As a skunk, Gram."

I notice Dad and Beth grouped in the doorway. Gram looks their way and swallows a smile. Dad returns it. "Are you hung over any?" she says, trying hard not to laugh now.

"I don't know, Gram. I haven't moved my head yet."

She and Dad are both grinning like crazy people, and Beth's thinking about it.

"All you look to me is hungry," Gram says. "I bet there's not a thing in your stomach."

"I can vouch for that," Dad remarks.

Gram goes into action. I love watching her go into action. She can turn on a dime. "Well, Beth, let's you and me fix this boy some breakfast before we go to work." They leave Dad with me, which may be the point.

Still keeping my head in place, I smooth a spot on the bed for him to sit down. "When's my court date, Dad?"

"You haven't got one."

"Do I still have a license?"

56

"It's over your visor. They were a pretty good bunch of guys down at the Evanston station."

"Evanston? What was I doing in Evanston?"

"You tell me."

I wish I could. "I see you're not too upset with me," I say instead.

"I don't get upset with you," Dad says, looking away, down at the floor. "You're a pretty good kid most of the time."

Then he looks back at me. "Of course you gave Beth a scare—that call from the cops in the middle of the night."

"Scare you any?"

"Maybe a little. But we had to get busy and come down to get you."

"Beth came with you?"

"Somebody had to drive your car home."

That's true. Somebody had to.

"Dad, it won't happen again."

"I don't expect it to," he says, looking away again. "And I'm not sorry it did. Something had to happen. You wouldn't grieve."

I move my head and look at him. "I grieved, Dad."

"No, you didn't know how, and I didn't know how to tell you. I didn't have the words. You didn't grieve. You just got quiet. That's the way I was when your mom died."

It's true, he doesn't mention her. And maybe I resent this some, because it makes it harder to remember her.

Besides, Dad always thinks what he has to offer isn't good enough. It's good enough for me. There's nothing wrong with this moment. In fact it's a pretty good moment, with Dad sitting here, doing a lot more talking than usual. And Gram and Beth out in the kitchen, and even the smell of bacon frying. I don't want any, but it smells good.

"Matt, do you think now maybe you can . . . stop looking back?"

"I doubt it. I love her, Dad."

He works his hands together, bunching up the knuckles. "I can understand that," he says. "I wasn't much older than what you are now when I . . . felt that way about your mom. You can't let it whip you, Matt. You do a lot of losing in life. You haven't lost your share yet."

"But, Dad, I lost what I never had. I loved Dory, but we never—I never made love to her."

He keeps working his hands. I'm really putting him through the whole course.

"Well, now," he says, "you don't have to go into—"

"I know I don't. But that's part of it, Dad. We were going to have so much. We were going to have it all. And now—nothing, for either of us."

He sits there on the side of the bed. I've put all my burden on him, and I still have it. The door opens. Gram's back, and Dad's glad to see her. He stands up, escaping, and starts for the door. When he gets there, he turns and gives me a broken smile.

"Thanks, Dad. It all helps."

Then Gram gives him a surprised look because he says, "A boy needs his dad."

Where did he get a line like that?

Chapter 8

It turns out to be a school day. I form a one-man chapter of Alcoholics Anonymous and go through the motions. School is this warm river that closes over my head and flows on. My body attends a few more days, but since I'd rather live in the past, things creep up on me. Surprises like spring vacation.

By the time Good Friday rolls around, I'm well on my way to a new solution. The seed was planted in that little talk Dad and I had. I'm about ready to put the past behind me, but school's not the environment for this. My plan forms. I'll iron out the details as I go. The first step is to get up to Juniper Lake.

The rest of the plan involves never coming back, not until this school year is over at least. I toy with the words *dropout* and *runaway*, but figure out ways to rephrase them. I'm not sure what a *sabbatical* is, but let's settle for *leave of absence*.

Let's also use the Easter vacation as the chance to

get away from home with a minimum of hassles. I can give them a phone call later. Once I'm up at the lake, things will fall into place. They're bound to. The main goal is to quit school.

But first I've got to get there. On Good Friday morning I wake up, ready to face the day for once. I shave, shower, shampoo, and announce my presence to the whole complex by blow-drying my hair with Beth's dryer, which sounds like a road grader.

While I'm stuffing a few changes into a flight bag, I hear through the walls Beth talking to Gram. She's dropped in again. She's dropping in a lot lately, hovering around to check on how I'm doing.

I pad into the kitchen to call Cal, giving him one more chance to tell me to come to work. But I've already done my stockroom work for the Easter rush, and he's been wanting to give me some time off ever since Dory died. He's about to give me a lot more time off than he knows.

No, he says, don't come in. Ron's here. I hang up and step, maybe too quick, into the living room, where I kill the conversation. I've been eavesdropping on it right through the phone call to Cal.

Hearing Beth say: ". . . He's just taking it too hard, Lola. Things aren't right with him, and I wonder if they ever will be. Wouldn't you think he'd begin to get over it?"

Gram: "Search me. I can't figure out kids these days. She was a real nice girl, wasn't she? I only met her that one time when they came in the store."

Beth: "Yes, I think she was, in her way. But no matter what she was, he's taking it too hard. I tried

60

to talk to him once, but I don't want him to feel I'm
. . . breathing down his neck. If his real mother was
alive, she—"

Gram: "Now don't go on like that. There's not a
thing she could do better than you."

A silence, and then Beth says, "Thank you for
that, Lola."

I enter, and they both jump. The spoon in Gram's
saucer leaps off and lands on her shoe. "Good grief,"
she says, twice as loud as before, "when did you stop
being so heavy-footed? Come over here, boy, and
give me a kiss."

I do, right under the earring. "What are you two
talking about?" I ask to fill in, because Beth and I
don't kiss.

"The weather." Gram pushes out her lips and
shifts gears on her bifocals at me.

"Matt?" Beth says. She's sitting in the Barca-
lounger, dressed for work and grabbing a peek at
her watch. "Where are you going with that bag?"

Here it comes.

"I'm going to take a run up to the lake." I shift
the bag from one hand to the other. "For a few days.
Easter break."

"You're what?" Gram overreacts for effect. "You're
not going to do any such a thing, Matt. We're going
to have a big Easter dinner. We don't all get together
enough as it is."

I see I'm handling this all wrong. Why did I leave
it till now?

"What I'd like to do," I say, "is to get away for . . .
a long weekend. I been kind of planning it."

Gram shoots a glance Beth's way. I think maybe I have them. Nobody's heard me say I've wanted anything, planned anything for quite a while.

But Gram only gives up in stages. "Now what do you want to go up there all by your lonesome for?"

"I like it up there. I always did, since back when I was little, and we'd come home on leave. When Grandpa was alive."

This is true, but probably not fair. I'm reminding her it was Grandpa's cottage, his and hers.

She reaches down and fishes up the spoon. She doesn't even like going up to the lake anymore, not without Grandpa. They built the place with their own hands, and Dad's, on a half-acre Grandpa got free with a newspaper subscription back when the lake was still a mudhole without a name.

"I like it up there, Gram. I have a lot of happy memories about that place."

She waits a minute and then says, "So do I."

Beth sees the way this conversation's going. "Matt, just stop by the plant and ask your dad if it's all right with him. I don't want him to come home and . . ."

"Beth, if I go ask Dad, he'll just say yes."

Gram's eyes roll behind the lenses. "That's the Lord's truth. Oh, go on, kid, and get out of here. We'll tell your dad for you."

I'm at the door by now, but Gram has a parting shot to fire. "You know what I wish, Matt? I'm going to tell you anyhow. I wish you was just a little tadpole of a kid again I could sit on my lap or turn over my knee."

I grin, and she makes two small fists to shake at

me. Then she gives me a pouty smile that invites Beth to do the same. My throat unclenches. I'm on my way.

I pull up into the yard in front of the cottage and sit there a minute, breathing real air and seeing the clouds upside down in the lake and the car hood. Now that I'm here, I'm not sure why. I seem to have been running from, not to. It hasn't occurred to me that I'm going to have to fill up the days here in my outpost.

I start by turning on the water in the cellar, hearing it gush through the pipes upstairs. Then I drag out the screens, hose them down, and start putting them up. The ladder shifts in slick new grass. I slip down three rungs before I find a footing. All I need is to break a leg and lie here for however long it takes to be discovered. I take a break and see a sunfish on the lake, its sail as small as a kite, but this is no real proof I'm not the sole survivor of some quiet catastrophe. Of course I could always go home, or crazy. Whatever works.

The screens are in, and the sun's beginning to sink down on the far side of the lake. I go for my shoes for a leisurely run: the 2.3-mile circuit over the roads. Before I'm out of the yard, I'm remembering how I came up here on the day of Dory's funeral. I've trapped myself into reliving that day.

On the incline up to the gravel road I get a stitch in my side, which ought to work out on the level stretch past the riding academy fence. I hit a reasonably controlled pace and hold it. The gravel begins to move under me in a steady way. The fence flashes past.

I'm halfway along now, and it begins to feel pretty good. My side unstitches. My throat's open, not too dry.

Off to the left there's a blur of blue beside the fence. It's a puddle reflecting the sky at first. Then it's something else, mysterious. A shape. As I move up on it, the form changes, possibly even moves. I'm thinking about it with only half my mind, using it as a marker. But the closer I get, the more it separates from the scene.

Then I'm walking, pulling in the air and blowing it out. The blue shape is half sunk in the ditch, screened by last year's tall grass. Somewhere up on a rise beyond the fence a horse stands, nuzzling the ground.

Trying to get my breath back, I walk up closer, hands on hips. And part the long grass with my Nike toe. Then I see her.

She's lying in the dry ditch—a girl. Or the ghost of one. I stop breathing and wonder if she has too. Her head's thrown back, and her eyes are closed above the line of her chin. But her neck's straight, unwrenched, and her arms are at her sides, one slightly bent. Her hands in smooth tight leather gloves hold fistfuls of rooted weeds in a grip. A death grip?

In this hallucination I'm having, she's wearing a tight-fitted short jacket that pinches her waist, and a long skirt, the same sky-blue, that goes all the way down to her ankles. It's a—what do you call it?—a riding habit. Nobody's worn one like it in years, maybe a century.

I'm not thinking. I'm just looking down her to where the end of the old-fashioned skirt turns back over narrow black riding boots.

She's a girl lying in a ditch, a girl from some other age. And she's as dead as . . . Dory.

The sweat in the small of my back goes cold just as the sun drops below the treetops, dimming the ditch. She's got to be dead, whoever she was. My foot retracts. I should go for help, except this may not be happening. I drop down on one knee and part the weeds again. I'm not going to touch her. I'm just going to make completely sure that—

Her eyes are open. They weren't before. She's looking down at me, crouched there by her bootheels. Her mouth opens, or her jaw drops down. She breathes out. Her gaze goes from dazed to sharp. She's staring holes in me. I couldn't run now if I had to, and she's trying to speak. Her chest heaves under the tight blue wool, and this seems to hurt her, because she grunts softly.

"Get . . ." she breathes.

"What?" I strain nearer to her, a little. I still don't believe this.

"Get . . . that . . . cockamamie . . . horse," she says.

"The what?"

Her eyes, dark blue with flecks in them, turn up to heaven. "Are you deaf?"

Her breath must be back, because she's fairly loud. I sit back on my heels.

"I said get that cockamamie horse." Trying to haul

herself up, she digs her elbows into the ground, freezes, and goes very white. In front of her left shoulder the blue wool looks swollen.

"Hold it!" I jump up, backpedaling for balance. "Don't move. I'll get your horse. Just stay where you are and don't—do anything."

Up the hill the horse, saddled, is chomping on grass, silhouetted against the sky.

I'm over the ditch in a mighty leap and hook a leg over the fence before I look back down on her. Yes, she's real and still there. "What'll I do with it when I get it?"

She hasn't moved much, except to roll onto her side. She sighs. "What do you think? Bring it down here and tie it to the fence."

She sighs again, totally exasperated at me. "Lead it down by the reins and tie the reins to the fence."

Her head droops. Her hair's spilling down out of a bun-thing on the back of her head. She gazes at the weeds. "The reins are those long leather ribbons."

"I know what reins are," I say from the top of my fence.

Trudging up the hill, I wonder what this horse is going to think of some human in a sweatsuit creeping up on him. What do I know about a horse? And this one could be deranged—a biter.

He keeps eating grass, and I grab at his reins, a distance from the teeth. He lets me lead him back to the fence, where I tie him to a post and finish off the job with a square knot.

"Give him some slack," the girl says, still looking at the weeds in the ditch. She's resting on her right side, and the bulge over her left shoulder looks bigger.

"Slack?"

"Slack."

I've tied a tight knot which takes some undoing. I give the reins some slack, and the horse, who's breathing all over my neck, drops his head and starts grazing again.

By the time I'm back over the fence, she's on her feet, picking burrs off her skirt. I don't quite know where to start with her. I'm still not a hundred percent sure she's real, though I'm pretty sure she has a temper.

I can't take my eyes off her outfit. Her skirt's full and even has a kind of train hung up on the weeds behind her. But I seem to know her legs are slim under the skirt. She's fussing one-handed with her hair, but it's mostly down now, nearly to her waist, and a somewhat horsy color—chestnut.

Since she's not looking at me, I'm looking at her. The outfit's distracting, but there's something modern about her face. Not pretty, but good—strong.

"Look," I say, "I mean—what happened?"

"What does it look like?" she asks, still picking burrs.

"It looks like you went over the fence and the horse didn't."

"Very funny," she says. "And true."

She looks at the horse. The saddle on it is nothing like I've ever seen. I don't see any stirrups, and it's got these horns curving out from it at odd angles. It doesn't even look like a saddle. In fact the horse looks like it's been unsuccessfully crossed with a unicorn. Things are getting weirder by the minute.

Chapter 9

She gives out a sigh, and the buttons on her jacket ripple with light. "I was riding the fence with him," she says, still exasperated. "I let him get too near it, and he brushed me off. He was just waiting his chance to do it, and he did it."

She looks at the sky with her flecked eyes.

"You took an incredible dive to land that way," I say. "You could have concussion."

"I remember going over the fence, and landing. Therefore—I don't have concussion. I only had the wind knocked out of me for a minute."

If she knows everything, I wish she'd explain more.

"I better get that nag back to the stable," she says. "I don't want them sending out a search party for him."

And you don't want them to know you took a fall either, but I don't say this. She's hitching up her fantastic skirts now, and climbing up the bank. Even I can figure out she doesn't want me to give her a hand. She swings her left arm out to grab the fence, but it's useless. It dangles there from her swollen shoulder. Her face is dead white.

"Just slow down. You hurt yourself."

"I couldn't have." But she knows she has. "When I fell, I threw out my arm behind me just before I hit the ditch on my back. I felt it, but . . . now I really feel it. But look, my fingers work."

The gloved fingers wiggle like mad at the end of her useless arm.

I'm looking up the bank at her, at the tears in her eyelashes. The swelling in her shoulder's getting worse. The shoulder could be busted, the arm broken in six places. What do I know?

"I'll take the horse back. You just wait, and then—"

"No." She's up on the fence, gasping with pain, and the sky's full of airborne skirt. Then she's down on the other side next to her friend the horse.

She's picking the knot loose, one-handed, and I let her. Who could stop her? Then she's taking charge of the horse again, maneuvering him to line up with the fence. I still can't figure out that saddle, but now she's back up on the fence and then up in the saddle somehow.

Under the settling skirt, her legs seem to be hooked in complicated ways around the horns. And finally I see, though I don't believe this either. She's sitting up on the horse with her back to me and both her legs going the other way. She's going to ride side-saddle.

I thought that whole thing went out with the

Civil War. This may even explain the old-time riding habit.

"What's this all about?"

She looks over her shoulder down at me. Way down. "What's what about?"

"Don't you ride with one leg on either side of the horse?"

"You mean cross-horse," she says.

"Whatever. Don't you?"

"Obviously not."

"But why? I mean, if you were riding—cross-horse, you probably wouldn't have fallen off."

"You mean that nobody who rides astride ever falls off?" Her voice drips with something. Venom, I think.

"No, I don't mean that, exactly. But—why do you do it?"

"Why do you run around in circles on country roads in that long underwear?" she asks.

Is this an answer? I change the subject. There's something gnawing at me. I don't want her to gallop off like the Queen of England in an old painting. I don't want her to gallop off at all.

"You coming back?" I say. "After you've stabled the horse?"

Her eyebrows rise. She's very cool up there against the sky. She wasn't cooler when she was out cold.

"Your shoulder's swelling, and your arm's hurting. You need to have somebody take a look at it." Then I play my big card. "You don't want anybody up at the stables to know you've bro—hurt yourself."

She doesn't. Her whole face says she doesn't. She jerks her head, which could mean anything, works the reins with one hand, turning the horse. Then, just to show me, she's going to take that hill at a gallop.

I point into the distance. "The fox went that way."

She gives me a sickeningly sweet smile, digs in a heel, and thunders off. If you could floorboard a horse, she just did it.

I wait. And wait. The road gravel's beginning to glow with evening.

Her head appears first, over the top of the hill. Her head and her hair caught by the breeze. It's a scene out of a very corny movie, and maybe this is what makes me think I've seen her a hundred times before. Her shoulders appear, squared. Then her arms, one dangling, the other one crooked to hold up her skirts, like she's carrying a little triangle of the sky. She's heading down the rise at a brisk stroll.

Leaning on the fence, I'd like to grin at this ridiculous, sort of wonderful impression she's making, but I'm not pushing my luck.

She climbs over, favoring her arm, and drops down beside me. "It got away," she says.

"The horse?"

"No. The fox."

I've laid a fire in the hearth and for once remembered to open the chimney damper first. There's an old pothook that Grandpa built into the fireplace, so I can boil water over the fire for instant coffee, if we have some, or tea, if I can find teabags. The gas hasn't been turned on, so the stove's useless. The electricity's off too, but we have the fire.

I'm banging around the kitchen, looking for mugs,

and she's sitting in the big room in front of the fire, her skirt tucked under her and fanning out.

We've been arguing. I haven't caught her name yet, but still, we've been arguing. I want to run her down to the hospital in the village and have them X-ray her shoulder. She's stalling, pretending it's only a bruise. Then she's saying there's no hurry; the emergency room's open all night. While I'm rummaging around in the pitch-black cupboards, she calls out, "Do you have a pair of scissors?"

I find them in the knife drawer and bring them out. The water's boiling over, threatening the fire. When I turn around, she's managed to cut the shoulder seam on her jacket, and it's already peeling down over the swelling, which is really huge.

"This is dumb. Let's just go down to—"

"Let's have some coffee first." She's putting things off like a little kid.

"It's tea."

"Fine. Sit down. You're making me nervous."

"You're nervous," I explain, "because you're afraid that when you get down to the hospital, they'll amputate your arm. Which they may do, if you don't get down there one of these days."

"I like this place," she says, looking around at the shadows the flames throw on the pine walls. She glances up at the wagon wheel light fixture that hangs down from a high beam. The cottage looks old, older than it is. She fits in here. The fire highlights her cheekbones.

"How long did you say you were lying in that ditch?" I settle down beside her.

She's concentrating on the fire, and her shoulder. "Five minutes, I suppose."

"Not longer? Not . . . years?"

She beetles her brows at me, and the shadows shift on her face. "This riding habit really blows you away, doesn't it?"

"To a certain degree."

"I'm beginning to see things from your limited viewpoint." She speaks over the rim of the mug. "You're having this fantasy that you've discovered Jane Eyre in a ditch."

"You said it. I didn't."

She smiles slyly into the fire. "I assure you that I occupy your time zone, more or less."

"Prove it."

She thinks. "Well, for one thing, I left the car up at the riding academy parking lot."

"Horseless carriage, you mean."

"You never give up, do you?"

It's night, and we're in the El Camino heading down to the village. The trees meet over the road, and the tunnel that forms in the summer is beginning to happen. It reminds me of the time Dory and I—

"You could just take me to my car. I could manage —really."

Still I keep not asking what her name is. Maybe Jane Eyre seems about right. And maybe I'm getting a small kick out of not knowing.

"What are you going to do, drive down into town one-handed, passing out from the pain?"

She's cradling her limp arm. "The pain isn't that

bad." We hit a bump, and she yelps. I pretend I don't hear, but she says, "Talk to me—about something else."

"Like what?"

"Anything. Your cottage."

"What can I tell you?" I say. "It's the greatest place there is. Even the way it smells. Pine needles and old ashes in the fireplace. I don't know how to say it. It's the safest place on earth."

She's listening to this pitch, so I go on. "We were sort of pioneers. When my grandpa first came up here, there wasn't another winterized cottage around. Just those little shacks they'd pull out onto the lake for ice fishing. I guess it's the only piece of property we own, so it's the place we can always get away to. But now civilization's creeping in."

The line of mailboxes looms up. And they prove the point, because some greaseball gang has smashed them all into junk metal, battered half of them off their posts. They really worked at it, and the ball bat they used lies in a rut in the road, splintered. I swerve to miss it.

She sees it all and says, "Civilization—you can't get away from it," summing up more than she knows.

Past the intersection we drive down the empty main street of the little town that's half for the lake people and half for farmers. The hospital emergency entrance sign looms up, and she moans quietly.

I pull in behind a paramedic van, and we make a fairly sensational entrance into the waiting room. A nurse takes one look at the sweatsuit-and-riding-habit combination and rolls her eyes at her buddies clustered

74

around a counter. An intern in a green smock turns around and does a double-take.

"Step right this way," he says to us. "The Halloween party's just beginning."

"Comedians," she wheezes out of the corner of her mouth, and lets him lead her away to an examining room, where a clinical-looking table is half visible.

I'm left in the empty waiting room with the nurse. She takes out a clipboard and dots a ball-point on her tongue. The interrogation begins. "You a relative?"

"No."

"Friend?"

". . . Not exactly."

She gives me a narrow look. The cap on her head looks like a white bat. "Name of the patient."

". . . Ah . . . I don't know."

She bangs her clipboard on the counter. "Look, I've got a job to do."

"I just found her," I say. "In a ditch. She sort of fell off a horse."

The nurse looks tired. "In that rig I didn't think she'd been hang-gliding. Hospitalization?"

"What?"

"Has she got Blue Cross, Blue Shield?"

"Beats me."

"It would. Does she have any I.D. on her? A purse?"

This is so ridiculous I'm beginning to enjoy it. "If she does, she's got it well hidden."

Something about this nurse makes me think she's about smart-mouthed enough to be enjoying it too. But, as she says, she has a job to do. She keeps making checks on a long form. "I don't suppose asking you her next of kin is going to get me far, is it?"

"Nope."

"Sit down."

I'm just turning when a shriek splits the air. Even Nurse Clipboard jumps. I can see into the examining room.

She's sitting up on the table, half draped in a sheet. Her head's thrown back. The intern's working at top speed, reeling off tape and looping it around her shoulder. Whatever's happened seems to be over. Her head falls forward, and the chestnut hair tangles in the tape.

I feel a little rocky myself until the intern swings out of the examining room.

"Shoulder," he says to the nurse. "A simple dislocation. And *pow*: I snapped it back into place with one deft manipulation."

"Trapper John lives," says the nurse, deadpan.

But the intern's delighted with himself. He pivots on his rubber sole and points at me. He should take up ballet. "You gonna take her home?"

"Don't ask him," says the nurse. "He hasn't known anything yet."

The intern isn't listening. He dances over my way and drops his voice. "There's a capsule around the shoulder joint," he explains, making a fist and covering it with his other hand. "She tore it in the fall. She's going to have to keep it immobilized for a while. I've got her in a sling that's pinned to her jacket, but she'll be fine. A little drowsy, though, because I've given her some medication for the discomfort."

Some discomfort. She's just been screaming. But now she's strolling out from the examining room, looking cool again. Ignoring the sling, she gives the nurse all the clipboard information while the intern reruns for me a couple of burn cases they've had from recent expressway pileups.

She seems to be handling the nurse. I notice she even borrows change for the pay phone. After she's made her call, she's by my side saying, "Let's go."

We're nearly out when the nurse yells after us, "You're going to call in your Blue Shield number, aren't you?"

She looks back, a queen again—on horseback. "Naturally."

We're heading out of town when she says, "*Now*, take me to my car. I'm not even sure if it's locked, and it's full of stuff."

"Out of the question. You're medicated. I'll take you home if you'll tell me where you live."

She seems to chuckle. "You really don't know, do you?"

"I really don't."

We're stopped for a light. "My name's Margaret, by the way. Margaret Chasen."

At last.

"My name's Matt Moran."

She just smiles at that. The light changes. "Margaret's a nice . . . old-fashioned name." I'm sorry, but it's all I can think of to say.

"My father picked it. From the poem, 'Spring and Fall: to Margaret.' 'Margaret are you grieving/Over

Goldengrove unleaving? . . .' It's by Hopkins. Do you know it?"

I shake my head.

"You would," says Margaret, "if you paid attention in Mrs. Tolliver's class. She does it every year."

The car swerves, leaps into oncoming traffic, fishtails back into our lane. "What do you know about Mrs. Tolliver's class?" This is too much.

"You're a junior, aren't you? So you probably have her third period."

My mind's gunning, in neutral. "Wait a minute," I blurt, though she seems to have all evening.

"Keep your eye on the road." She knows I was about to give her a long, searching look that could send the car up the nearest tree. But I don't even have to, because there's been something familiar about her all along. I've seen her before, a lot. I don't know her, but I know that face, and it's fairly memorable.

"It's that crazy outfit you're wearing," I explain.

"Maybe."

"And finding you sort of unexpected by the side of the road, like a—hedge apple."

"Possibly," Margaret says.

"I don't know why I didn't recognize you—I mean I do, but I just didn't—"

"I'm a senior," Margaret says, "if that helps."

It doesn't much. Seniors are more noticeable than anybody else. "It's a factory," I say. "That school. Totally impersonal, like the rest of Glenburnie. Everybody's in a little group and never even looks up. A bunch of zombies walking through the whole experience."

"Are you describing yourself?" Margaret asks.

78

Maybe I am, since she doesn't seem to fit into this category. But it's rough not knowing somebody who knows you unless you're on a team or something. We've come to the blinker light that signals the road up to the lake.

"Listen," I say, "how did you happen to recognize me?"

"I've seen you around school," Margaret says. "You're a pretty good-looking kid—for a junior."

I decide to change the subject. "I want to take you home." I'm being reasonable, sensible. "I guess you must live in Glenburnie, but are you staying up here at the lake, or what? And let's get one thing straight right now. I'm not taking you to your car, because you're not supposed to drive tonight."

"Is that all you have to say?"

"For the moment."

"Yes, I live in Glenburnie. I was planning to drive back tonight. I've got a carload of—"

"Well, you're not going to."

"I know," she says. "I'm medicated."

We bomb off, heading for the expressway entrance. I feel sort of medicated myself: a little overpsyched or something. If she needs to sleep, she ought to, but I wish she wouldn't.

I'm still searching my brain to place her. There's something of Glenburnie Woods about her, but not quite.

"We live on Sycamore," she says, reading my mind. It isn't even close to Glenburnie Woods.

"No kidding? We used to live on Hawthorne."

"Where do you live now?"

Aha. Finally there's something she doesn't know.

But why is this a slight letdown? "Camelot Close on Beltline." And then I add: "Not exactly the life-style Glenburnie's famous for."

With the hand on her good arm she arranges the folds of her skirt. "I wasn't sure," she says, but what that means she doesn't say.

The expressway's nearly empty both directions. I don't want to talk her head off, but . . . "Now then, about this Jane Eyre business."

She rolls her head back against the seat. But she's wide awake. "I ride at Ritchey's Riding Academy because they have off-season rates, and I need all the practice I can get."

"Then you don't own the horse."

"That hayburner?" She bristles. "If I did, he'd be library paste by now."

I chuckle dutifully. Besides, it's not a bad line. "So much for the horse. Now about the—"

"Sidesaddle," she says. "I know, I know. You thought the sidesaddle went out with powdered wigs—"

(That's near enough.)

"—but you're wrong. Actually women rode aside into the twentieth century. In fact," she says, warming up now, "a woman rode aside in the Virginia hundred-mile trail ride as late as 1960. Won first prize too. Want to know her name?" She starts to dig me with her elbow, but it's the wrong one.

"Not particularly. Just go on with your own story."

"It's simple. Riding aside is coming back. It's graceful. It respects the past. It requires a specialized expertise, which I'm working on, and—"

"And you like being different."

80

"Do you have any objections to that?"

"No."

Then she's quiet while she's thinking about believing me. "Besides, it isn't different. There's a club of women who ride aside, who meet out west of Wheaton. I joined last fall, and I'm in hock up to my ears paying for this habit, which I have to practice in. Otherwise I'll never be able to handle the skirt. The club does precision riding, so it's got to look right—and be right."

"And where do you find a saddle like that?"

"I picked it up for practically nothing at a barn sale up here just over the state line."

"They were selling a barn?"

She sighs. "They were having a sale in the barn. In the suburbs it's garage sales. In the country it's barn sales."

"Oh. You go to barn sales a lot?"

"That's my business."

"Sorry."

"No, I mean that's my *business*."

She's in business? I thought she was a senior. A couple of miles tick over on the odometer before I think of something to say. "You mean all those women in that club have to find their sidesaddles at barn sales?"

"No. I was lucky. In fact, finding the saddle got me interested in riding. If you've got the money, you can have one custom-made by a saddler. Or you can get a used one sometimes through an ad in our national magazine, which is called—"

"*Sidesaddle News*," I offer, taking a shot in the dark.

81

She stiffens. "Yes. You're getting a big bang out of this, aren't you?"

"No." And since we're driving along in the dark—and maybe because I haven't really talked to anybody for a long time, I say, "I wouldn't laugh at it, because it looks great. Even just the glimpse I got of you sitting the horse like women did for centuries. I don't know how to put it. I can see it'd be very satisfying."

"It is," she says. "It's linking up a part of the past with the present. Who wants to be locked into anything—even a time?"

I hadn't given it much thought.

"By the way," she says, "I see you're not the complete put-down artist after all."

"Far from it. I'm going to be a big fan of yours when you're famous around school for winning some trail ride like Mrs. What's Her Name from Virginia, or—"

"My opportunities for fame around school are pretty limited," she says. "I graduate in June."

That's right. She's a senior. She's also asleep. That medication really takes hold. In the light from an oncoming car I catch a glimpse of her head thrown back and a small bubble forming on her lips.

In another half hour we're driving through what's left of downtown Glenburnie, past the boarded-up train station and the empty shells of stores moved to the mall. Then, after I've found Sycamore Street, I have to wake her to ask her which block, which house.

"Margaret?"

She does what you do when you're pretending you

haven't been asleep. We're stopped under a street-
light, and I'm enjoying this performance, especially
when she looks down, surprised at the sling.

"Oh! Yes. I live—where are we? Yes, the next
block, third house. The porch light's on." She sits up
straight. "I'm really sorry to drag you all the way
back down here. Were you planning to spend the
weekend at the lake?"

"I had no plans, Margaret. Believe me."

She seems to.

"I guess you'll have to get your car back from up
there."

She nods. "We call it the Rusty Rabbit. My dad
said we'd have to drive up tomorrow and get it."

Suddenly I want to know about her family, about
everything. But it's too late. "You told your dad you
weren't driving the—Rusty Rabbit back home?"

We're stopped in front of her porch light. She
turns large eyes on me. "I told him you'd be bringing
me home."

She told him that on the phone at the hospital. And
after that she was still telling me to take her to her
car.

Now she's slipping away, and I know I'm not
supposed to go up to the door with her.

I drive home, just comfortably tired. And I manage
to get from the parking lot to my bed without disturb-
ing Dad or Beth. They don't even discover me till
next morning. Gram and Beth say they're glad I
decided to come home for Easter, and I think Dad is
too. Everybody's glad I had a change of heart.

Chapter 10

I add dropping out to liquor on my growing list of failed solutions. And I'm back at school for no particular reason.

And searching the halls from early morning on. It's not going to surprise me much if I don't recognize her. Maybe it shouldn't surprise me if she doesn't exist, though I've pretty well worked through that fantasy. Besides, there are Chasens in the phone book, on Sycamore.

I live through Contemporary Social Issues and a free period on the way to Mrs. Tolliver's BritLit. I've been slipping behind too much lately. Now I have to —take a different tack.

You don't catch up in a single hour though. We're still doing poetry—nineteenth century. But I'm lost in a blizzard of Xerox sheets and a blank notebook. Dory's class notebooks were incredible. She even numbered the pages and added footnotes.

The bell rings during my paper-shuffling, and the room clears out. Since lunch follows, I move up to Mrs. Tolliver's desk, where she's sitting, pulling out a brown bag. She looks up, fairly receptive.

"Bring your lunch?" she says.

I shake my head.

"Mind if I?" She holds up her brown bag. I sit down in a front seat, not my usual location. Mrs. Tolliver's rooting around in her bag for a sandwich, smiling a little. She has small smiles, a long oval face, plain clothes.

I don't know how to talk to a woman who can live in a world of poetry. "About this poem," I say. "It's about . . . leaves falling . . ."

She thinks.

"By Father Hopkins." She puts down the sandwich, peels the lid off a tub of yogurt, and dips in a plastic spoon.

"I think so."

"We read that about two weeks ago," she says. "In class."

We did?

"I guess it had a . . . delayed effect on me."

"That's what poetry's for." She stirs a whirl in the yogurt.

"Could we—maybe go over it again?"

"In class?" she asks.

"No. Now?" I'm sitting here with my legs all over the floor, jammed into this desk seat, asking a teacher to read poetry to me on her lunch hour.

"I don't think I have any more sheets," she says. "Do you have yours?"

"Mrs. Tolliver, I don't know if I have it or not."

"It's all right," she says, laying her sandwich aside. "The truth is, I know the poem by heart, but I'm putting you off. Speaking Hopkins's poetry requires a certain—technique—"

A specialized expertise, I think, picking the phrase out of the air.

"—and I'm not really very good at it."

I edge back in my chair. "If you wouldn't mind, Mrs. Tolliver, you're going to be good enough for me."

She dips her head, and I can see her when she was young and still somewhat shy. She begins: " 'Margaret are you grieving/Over Goldengrove unleaving? . . .' "

Yes, that's the one.

" 'Leaves, like the things of man, you
With your fresh thoughts care for, can you?
Ah! as the heart grows older
It will come to such sights colder
By and by, nor spare a sigh
Though worlds of wanwood leafmeal lie; . . .' "

She stops. "What do you see so far?" she says, meaning in the poem that's still hanging unfinished in the air.

"Sugar maples," I say, taking a crack at it. "A grove of maple trees bright yellow in the fall— golden."

"And?"

"And a girl—Margaret. Maybe a little girl, standing in front of the trees, crying."

"Why?"

"Because . . . they're beautiful, but the leaves are falling, so it's all going to be over pretty soon."

Mrs. Tolliver looks out the window and goes on:

> " 'And yet you will weep and know why.
> Now no matter, child, the name:
> Sorrow's springs are the same.
> Nor mouth had, no nor mind, expressed
> What heart heard of, ghost guessed:
> It is the blight man was born for,
> It is Margaret you mourn for.' "

She's finished now, so I have to say something. "That part's harder. This girl's crying over the trees losing their leaves, but somebody's telling her she's crying over something else. That she's crying not because the trees are dying, which they aren't, but because she'll die one day herself. And maybe it's just dawned on her."

"And this is pessimistic?" Mrs. Tolliver asks. "Hopeless?"

"No. The poet—somebody's telling her it's what she has in common with everybody. It just *is*. I'm not even close, am I?"

"Of course you are," she says. Then she breaks the mood by picking up her sandwich. Her timing's good. This much I've noticed about her before. And she doesn't ask why I've plucked this particular poem out of the large pile that have gotten by me over these past weeks since—

I start to unwedge myself from the desk.

"Poetry intimidates me," I say.

"No, it doesn't," Mrs. Tolliver says and nods to the door, helping me through it.

And after I've spent most of the morning looking for her, for Margaret, she finds me in the cafeteria. I'm sitting there hunched over a pizzaburger with Father Hopkins and his poem, which I've found misfiled in my chemistry workbook.

A tray appears above me, held one-handed. A tray and a sling. My head jerks up, almost butting the tray out of her hand.

"Pardon me," she says in a stage whisper, "but I just fell off this horse, and I wonder if you'd mind if I sat down."

"What? Oh, sure. Listen . . . hi."

I'm cool, suave. Melted cheese spatters all over the poem page.

She sits down next to me, sliding her tray with a hand already practiced. Her other arm rides easy in its sling. "Do you usually eat in the cafeteria?" I say, looking around at the lonely crowd.

"Usually," Margaret says. "At a senior table."

"That's probably why I haven't noticed you here."

"Maybe."

She reads the title on the poem I've forgotten to keep covered by my arm.

"What a coincidence," she says, making big round eyes. "You happen to be doing the Hopkins poem in Tolliver's class today." Margaret pokes a fork at the Xerox sheet. "She did hand these out today, didn't she?"

"Yeah. Talk about a coincidence."

"You wouldn't lie to me, would you?" Margaret wonders.

"Maybe just a small one."

"How do you like the poem?"

"It's a definite down," I say, "now that I think about it. Look at the words: *weep, sorrow, mourn*— even *blight*."

Margaret's been demolishing a plate of macaroni and cheese, but now she's staring at me like the first moment we met.

"I mean," I say, "I can see why you'd like it because it's where your name came from. But how come all poetry has to whimper and whine about dying and death?"

"It doesn't," she says, "and I'm sure you know that."

She drops her fork and takes up a napkin to dab at her chin. Her whole right side is moving like a piston engine. The bell rings, rattling all the glassware, and she's reaching down for a book bag. Time's run out again, and I've made the usual fool of myself.

"Listen," I say, "why don't we get together and— talk about this poem?"

She's on her feet now, kneeing her chair back against the table, looping the strap of the book bag over her good shoulder.

"Because we wouldn't be talking about a poem. We'd be talking about Dory Gunderson."

Chapter 11

I make it through two more days, and nights. And I don't see her around school, but then I'm not looking up much. I go along from class to class, counting the squares in the floor tile. I'm making a pretty good adjustment to being miserable. I may be able to make a lifetime career out of it.

And on Wednesday I work an extra night for Cal. He and Ron haven't sold all the Easter merchandise they'd hoped to, so I have a lot of reticketing to do with new sale prices—amazing reductions.

Ron comes back to the stockroom for his closing-hour Kent Light. He's into a new look tonight. Slicked-back hair. An oatmeal-colored sport coat, very narrow lapels. Inch-wide knit tie. And from the headless dummy the tattersall shirt that didn't sell.

He flicks a disposable lighter. "Man, we couldn't give it away tonight. I mean, naked people were coming in with credit cards in their hands and wouldn't buy fig leaves." Smoke shoots up to the rafters.

"Father's Day's coming," I mention, to raise his spirits.

He throws an arm over his face, rocks back on the wrapping table. "Satin ties," he moans. "The lowest moment of the year."

"Do you know Margaret Chasen?" I slash a price with a red ball-point, hoping to catch Ron off guard.

He looks at me, but I'm busy taking twenty percent off everything.

"Fairly tall. Foxy. Long, kind of auburn hair?"

"Like that," I say. I put a couple of pins in my mouth. I keep working.

"I know who she is," Ron says, which is obvious. "And I figure anybody that cool isn't worth the aggravation."

Ron likes his women humble, and plain. "I'd keep my distance." He flips ash off his pleated pants.

From the mall I drive downtown and then up Sycamore. It's only about twenty-two blocks out of my way. Keeping my distance, I drive past her house. The porch light's off, but other lights are on, upstairs and down.

Making a right at the corner, I swing back around the block. The houses are close and not new, filling up their lots, leaving small front yards. They even have alleys. The neighborhood's more like a real town than a suburb. I seem to be driving past her house again.

This time I notice the outline of a junior-size bicycle lying across the front steps. I brake at the corner, sit there a full minute in case there's cross traffic. The whole town's deserted, but still I practice good driving habits. And swing around the block again. It's about time for me to go home.

In fact I mean to, but the El Camino's driving itself around the block on its own. I let it, creeping past her house one last time. Then I see somebody standing out in the street. As the headlights pick him up, he puts his arms out like a school crossing guard.

A tall, rangy guy with very thin hair and hollow cheeks. He's wearing a dress shirt and jeans and what look like carpet slippers. His hands are still out, and he's looking up to keep from being blinded. I stop.

He comes over to my side. I suppose this could be a citizen's arrest.

"You Matt?"

I nod. There's something dreamlike about all this.

"Before you wear out the pavement," he says, "just pull in the drive." He thumps the car door, points to the driveway, the Chasens' driveway.

What am I going to do? Floorboard it and get out of here? Burn rubber? I swing into the drive. There's a car parked there and another in the garage. The one in the open is a Rabbit—rusty.

I sit there, wondering what happens next. He looms up at my wing window. "We don't give curb service. Come in the house." Then he waits while I climb out of the car.

"Look, I'm sorry. I didn't mean to bother you."

"Me?" His shoulders inch up into the night. "I

didn't even know you were out here. Don't worry about it. Come on in."

I follow him around to the front. On the porch steps I notice training wheels on the bike. The mystery deepens. Except not actually. This has got to be Margaret's father, and whatever's coming next has got to be really embarrassing.

He holds the screen door open for me. I think he's getting a kick out of this. Off the front hall is what should be the living room, but it doesn't look quite like one. There's a slab sofa with an afghan on it. A coffee table with a Monopoly board on it half through a game. Puzzle parts and Scrabble tiles all over the shag rug.

An old knee-hole desk slants across the corner. Anybody sitting there could see out to the street. Margaret's sitting there with her slinged arm pinned to her shirt.

She looks up. "Hello, Matt. Good-bye, Daddy."

He chuckles behind me and heads off down the hall toward the light of a kitchen. I stand there trying to absorb this room while I get ready to face Margaret. Around her desk is a big jumble of packing boxes full of unidentifiable junk. It looks like moving day, except she doesn't move. Her desk is covered with homework and other things too: blank price tags and that plastic bubble stuff you pack breakables in. The whole place is in a state of advanced chaos. Margaret looks calm. Her hair's pulled back with a ribbon. She's wearing jeans and no shoes. Has she kicked the riding habit?

"Isn't the parking situation around here murder?" She makes big eyes.

I shuffle in the shag. "I was just driving around."

"And around," she says, "and around and around and a—"

"Knock it off, Margaret. Put me out of my misery. Think of me as a horse."

"I already am," she says. "Guess which end of the horse I'm visualizing."

"This isn't funny, Margaret," I say in a level tone, clenching up my teeth a little. "Did you send your dad out—there?" I jerk my head toward the street.

She points at herself. "Me?" Her eyes are big again, a very annoying trait. "No. He goes out there every night and flags down cars. He tests brakes for a hobby. Have a seat." She looks at the sofa behind the Monopoly set.

What can I do? My cover's already blown. I edge along behind the coffee table, past Baltic Avenue, Park Place, the Reading Railroad. I pass Go and don't collect $200.

She's turned her chair around. "Sit all the way down."

"You really like having the upper hand, don't you?" I probably shouldn't have said that, because she actually only has one functioning hand at the moment, but she ignores the remark anyway.

"I was just doing a little homework," she says. "You've heard of homework."

While I'm thinking up an answer, a short, fat little kid shows up in the doorway to the hall. About eight years old with a red-striped rugger shirt straining around his belly. There's an open area between the shirt and his pants like a large, fleshy pink smile. He peers into the room through deep-buried eyes.

"Well, Jason," Margaret says, "what can we do for you?"

Fat Jason scans the room, trying to decide. "I want my game."

"Monopoly?"

"Yes." Jason realizes that he could pick up the Monopoly board in one swoop and wouldn't have an excuse for hanging around. "No.

"Scrabble," he decides. The tiles are all over the room. It could take him a month to collect them all.

"Right," Margaret says. "And after you've got all of them, you can start on the jigsaw parts."

If the kid's reasonably bright, he'll see she's calling his bluff. He drops down on the rug and starts picking the Scrabble tiles out of the rug, turning each one over in his hand.

Margaret gives me a look that seems to say, *Keep talking.*

Which is fine, except I couldn't think of anything to say even before this kid started rooting around on the floor.

". . . How's the shoulder?"

"I've been to a real doctor," she says, "who told me, 'Time is the great healer' and charged me thirty dollars."

"Oh."

Jason's on all fours, collecting tiles across the floor between us. He looks like a swollen mole, and he's all ears.

"And something else," Margaret says. "I have to retire from the sidesaddle club. The shoulder's going to be too stiff, and I can't get the practice in to do precision riding this season."

"That's too bad." The vision of her in her old-fashioned outfit up on the horse starts to fade. I'm sorry to see it go. But then, she looks just as good to me in regular clothes, and a lot more real.

"I liked it well enough to go back to it someday."

She's been talking directly over Jason's head. It occurs to him that picking up every loose object on the floor is work. He scoots his sausage legs around and sits up. Tiles spill out of his hands.

"Who is this anyway?" he says to Margaret, angling a thumb my way.

"It's Matt."

"What's he doing here?"

"He's on a secret mission."

Jason gives me a beady look. His eyes almost disappear. Margaret leans nearer his ear. "We're going to run away together, so don't tell Daddy."

The kid's eyes bug out. He's up in a crouch, panting as his weight shifts. Then he's out of the room, moving at sensational speed, heading for Daddy. This is not a very bright kid, and Margaret knows just how to deal with him.

"Now then, where were we?" she asks.

"Frankly, I don't know. I guess I wanted to stop by and see you, but—"

"I'm glad you did." She works her toes in the rug. "The other day in the cafeteria—we didn't exactly end on the right note. I shouldn't have—"

"Mentioned Dory? You were right. I'd probably work her into any conversation. She's still in my mind a lot. In fact, I—want her to be. I don't want to lose what's left. She's already beginning to fade, and that hurts."

Margaret says nothing, examines her sling.

"I guess I ought to be working it out on my own," I say. "That's probably the thing to do."

"It probably isn't. I expect you should talk it out with somebody. It's just that I wouldn't care to play the role," she says. "I'm not such a bad listener, but I don't know if I want to hear about it."

Jason pounds up the hall from the kitchen and swerves up the stairs. "Now," Margaret says, "he's going to tell his mother about us. Before she gets through explaining to him he's been had, I figure we've got another five minutes."

I look down at the Monopoly dice, turned up snake eyes, and wonder if we've got five minutes' worth of anything left to say.

Rubbing my hands together, I show a little enthusiasm. "How about this. How about us getting together once in a while and not talking about . . . anything in the past."

She's shaking her head. "It wouldn't work. If you put a subject off limits, it crops up every two seconds."

While I'm trying to work around this reasoning, a firm foot is heard on the stairs, and it isn't Jason's scuttle. A woman appears at the doorway and glances in. She's sort of heavy, with Jason's round cheeks propping up rimless glasses.

"Oh, hello there," she says to me.

I start to get up, but I'm going to knock over the Monopoly board.

"Jason won't be troubling you anymore tonight. I sent him to bed," she says to Margaret, giving her a bleak look. Then she vanishes.

97

"She must have talked fast," Margaret remarks. "I make it about three minutes."

I'm not sure whether I'm welcoming these interruptions or not.

"We're not very big on introductions around here," she says. "You met my father in the street. And you've met my stepbrother."

"Stepbrother?"

She nods. "No blood relation. There's no family resemblance, is there?"

"Absolutely none," I say, fast.

"My parents got divorced when I was about twelve. I see my mother about twice a year out in California. They were fairly liberal, so they let me decide which parent I wanted to live with. Being that age, I thought it would be great to get away from my mother. So I got a stepmother instead. You don't think far enough ahead when you're twelve."

"I've got a stepmother too," I say, uncovering a bond between us.

"Like mine?" Margaret says, big-eyed.

"Not too much. No."

A thumping sound comes from the ceiling. Jason must be directly overhead, gathering up a bunch of Mars Bars to take to bed.

"I haven't been around many little kids, except Dory's little sister, Ruth—"

My tongue freezes, a moment too late. Silence takes over the room. And so does Dory.

Margaret just shrugs. It may mean *I told you so.* I reach down and give the dice a flick. "I better get going."

"Why?"

"Why not?"

"Because," Margaret says, "the next time you come around, I won't send Daddy out to the street to haul you in."

I'm up and edging around the Monopoly board. "No, listen, I think I ought to go."

"Why don't you take me out and buy me a root beer," she says.

"You really want to go?"

"I really want to go."

We drive all the way over to Green Bay Road before we find anything open that isn't a McDonald's. And then all we find is a pancake house.

So we decide to split a stack of strawberry pancakes and work through a monster pot of coffee. I try to make the pancakes last and watch the whipped cream substitute turn into blue water on the plate. Then I torture three paper napkins to death.

"So," I say. Brilliant.

"So?"

"So it's funny. We go to the same school, but we probably never would have met there."

"You said yourself the other night that school's a totally impersonal factory. I think you also mentioned it's full of zombies. Maybe you meant vampires. They sleep all day."

"I said all that?"

"That seemed to be your main meaning, as far as I could tell."

"It's true, though, isn't it?"

99

"It's true if you think it's true." She's stirring coffee slowly with her good hand. She's bored with me. I'm practically sure of it.

A bunch of kids come past our booth. Very preppie and dead-eyed. Probably from New Trier.

Finally Margaret says, "Why don't you just tell me all about her?"

"You've already said you didn't want to hear about her."

"I wasn't thinking far enough ahead again," she says.

"You thought about that. How come you don't want to hear about her?"

"If you'd ever really known two girls in your life, you'd know that one doesn't especially like hearing about the other one."

"Even if she's . . . dead?"

"Especially then."

"So let's drop the subject."

"No. Tell me about her," Margaret says. "My ego's not involved. You and I aren't quite friends, and we're not quite strangers. We're not quite anything. So talk."

"You probably knew her anyway," I say.

"More or less. Like anybody who wasn't in her group."

"I wasn't in her group either, and they were pretty tight with each other."

"Did they take you in?"

"I guess they did what Dory wanted."

"What were they like?"

"Oh, I don't know. They didn't hang out. Pretty much above it all. One thing that kind of surprised me was that they didn't do too much except get together on the weekends at somebody's house. They were kind of like a family for each other. It was nice in a way. They had a reputation as the top bunch, so I figured there'd be at least a couple of burn-outs and some fairly wild behavior. But it wasn't like that. They—we sat around and talked a lot in people's family rooms. Maybe listened to some music."

"Did they ever come to your house?"

"No. They kept pretty much to Glenburnie Woods. I don't think they knew anyplace else."

I see something in Margaret's eyes, I'm not sure what.

"I wasn't ashamed to have them come to my house. I didn't think about it."

There's still something in her look that bothers me.

"Dory came up to the lake once. And one time when we were just driving around, we stopped at the store where my grandmother works. She's at the A & P on the check-out counter."

I'm not sure why I'm telling this, or even why I'm remembering it.

"Dory and I got in line like regular customers—we were buying Doritos or something. But I made sure we were in Gram's line, and when we got up to her, I introduced the two of them. I don't think Dory believed it at first, but then Gram leaned across the counter and kissed me—planted a big one on my ear."

Silence at the end of this great saga. "And?" Margaret says.

"And I think it grossed Dory out that I had a

grandmother who checks out groceries. It's funny in a way. Gram lived in this town before it was a suburb. A long time before there was a Glenburnie Woods."

I see now what I've said. I've sold Dory out, and it didn't take me long. I've made her sound like a spoiled brat and maybe worse. It's time to leave. Past time.

In the car, in the dark, I say, "You think Dory was a snob, don't you?" I look over at Margaret, at her profile.

"You were doing the talking," she says in a tired voice.

"I know. But still—"

"I don't think she was any more of a snob than anybody else," Margaret says. "I think she was conventional."

"Conventional?" What kind of a word is that? "Meaning?"

"Meaning that she was just what she was and like everybody else she knew. I don't happen to want to be like that, so she isn't a threat to me. But then, she's not very interesting to me either, so that's why I'm not a very good listener. She meant too much to you. She can't mean enough to me."

I suppose that's clear enough, but I don't want to accept it.

"You said that you and I weren't quite friends. Do you think maybe we could be?"

Margaret thinks a long minute, and I drive a little slower.

"You might not want me for a friend. Friends sometimes tell you things for your own good."

"Like what?"

"Like why don't you stop feeling sorry for yourself? You can't see anything or anybody but Dory. She's got a bigger hold on you now than when she was alive. And you're going around in this . . . fog of self-pity."

"I'm trying to get over that," I say. "Why don't you want to help me? I'm trying to reach out to you."

"No. You're trying to reach back to her."

"You've got an answer for everything, Margaret."

We're stopped at a light, and all I can manage is a drum roll with my jittering thumb on the bottom of the steering wheel.

"It looks like you and I are over before we've even started."

For a while Margaret doesn't say anything, which must mean she agrees. And then she looks my way and says, "I think that woman in the next car knows you."

There's a Buick pulled up beside us on my side, waiting for the light. The woman next to the driver looks straight into my eyes; then she leans forward to see Margaret. She turns her head away, toward her husband at the wheel. The light changes, and I let the Buick pull ahead of us. She knew me all right. It was Dory's mother.

Chapter 12

"Lady up front to see you," Cal says, poking his head through the curtain into the back room, where I'm steam-pressing seersucker suits. Ron's overseeing my labor on his break and just naturally eases off the wrapping table and shoots his cuffs.

"Not you," Cal says with an evil leer. "Lady to see Matt."

I barely hear this through the hiss of steam as I flatten seersucker. It's a Saturday afternoon of sudden summer coming in May: eighty degrees outside and a hundred and ten in here.

"Old lady? Young lady? Fox lady? Lady in distress? What type lady?" Ron says, a little too loud if you ask me.

"Young. Foxy," Cal says, "but not for you, Ron." His head disappears.

Since I'm pretending deafness, Ron makes a sweeping gesture toward the door. After several days—more than a week—all right, ten days exactly, it must be Margaret. And she wants to see me

"I'm not going out front," I tell Ron. "Look at me. I'm wringing wet and stink like a pig."

"Honest sweat," he says. "It may be a turn-on. Give it a shot."

I don't need any more smart talk, so I leave the steam presser gaping open and start for the front, mopping my brow. I'm not going to know what to say to her. I never do. I've given up on her.

I slip through the curtain, trying to look busy, interrupted. The store's practically empty, but still I don't spot her. In fact there's only a tall, slender blonde standing up by the front door, against the glare from the afternoon sun.

It's nobody like Margaret. She wouldn't stand barely inside a door, poised for flight.

I walk nearer and see it's Linda Whitman. Linda of the Dory and Carol and Linda trio. I don't think I've ever seen her on her own. Dory was always there and did most of the talking for both of them.

"Linda?"

"Matt. Hi." She smiles and looks down. I sense Cal hovering somewhere behind us.

"So what's happening?"

"Well, look at me." She turns out scrubbed white palms, presenting herself. She's wearing a work shirt with the tails knotted at her waist and jeans with floppy legs too long. Her narrow, shoeless dancer's feet peer out from under ragged cuffs. And she's dripping wet, as wet as I am. Even her hair's soaked and darkened, curling up tight against her head. This is not Linda's perfect grooming, though she's wearing a gold chain around her neck.

"We're having a car wash down at the end of the parking lot. It's a fund raiser for the junior dance next week."

The junior dance has slipped my mind, if it was ever in it. What does she want me to do, have my car washed?

"How's business?"

"Oh, fine." Her head bobs. "We were only about a hundred dollars short, and we'll make that."

"That's . . . great."

"Matt, why don't you come down and join us?"

"Who's there?"

"Everybody. Carol, Todd, Jay—you know, everybody."

It sounds like the Glenburnie Woods shock troops, with maybe a few token underlings thrown in to make it a class project.

"I don't get off till five, Linda."

"Take off!" Cal says, loud and near. Linda and I both leap. She smiles again and glances down at the puddles forming around her feet.

"I've got some work to finish up, but I'll drop by later."

"I wish you would," she says, and gives me a cautious look in case I'm only trying to weasel out.

And in another half hour I clock out early to keep Cal off my case. I wave at him from the door as I leave.

"Good!" he yells over from the shaving lotion counter. "Get out and have some fun for once."

"You're the perfect boss, Cal. You're going to spoil me for real life."

"Get outa here," he says, pretending to lob a bottle of Brut at me.

I see the junior class car wash down at the end of the lot, just this side of the regular Saturday flea market. And I see by their sign they're getting three bucks a pop. They're working over a new Mercedes, and waiting next in line is Royce Eburt's silver Porsche, with Royce at the wheel and Sheri Martinson curled up beside him. They're even getting seniors for customers.

Carol MacIntosh in painter's pants soaked to her curves is turning a hose on Todd and Jay. She's squealing; they're dancing backward. The Mercedes is getting a wash as an afterthought. Sitting on her heels, Linda manages to look graceful as she polishes a hubcap. A couple of other people, possibly classmates of mine, are starting on Royce's Porsche. He's already out of the car, in no danger from Carol's hose, telling them how to handle his windshield wipers.

This isn't a party I particularly care to crash, but Linda's caught sight of my reflection in the hubcap and turns around.

"Look who's here," Todd says.

"The widower returns," Jay remarks. But Carol's at his side, digging him in the ribs to shut him up. Carol must be taking over the leadership role now, and Linda's beginning to follow her like she followed Dory.

Life's going on for them, though Carol's working overtime on her squeals. Somebody hands me a chamois, and I pitch in, one of the gang again. I also

107

know a little more about wiping down a car than they care to.

The extra careful job we do on Royce's Porsche nearly satisfies him. And by now Jay and Todd have walked over toward the flea market to pass a joint back and forth. They're being reasonably discreet about it, and they aren't offering a drag to Linda and Carol because nice Glenburnie Woods girls don't.

"I can smell that stuff from here," Carol says, wrinkling up her nose. "I hate it. You don't smoke grass, do you, Matt?"

"I have no vices," I say, and Carol nods approvingly. Only Linda catches the irony and smiles.

Todd and Jay are ambling back, not noticeably higher than before. "We're in the wrong business," Todd says. "Do you know what they're getting for all that junk at the flea market? Megabucks. Petrodollars."

It's probably true. The Saturday flea market makes a bigger haul in the parking lot than the shops in the mall.

"And it's all tax-free," Jay says. "This country's going to be back to the barter system before you know it. Big government makes criminals of us all." He's an executive of tomorrow and already a worried man.

"Can you imagine sitting out here with all those . . . people in that hot sun trying to sell used Tupperware, or something?" Carol says. "I'd rather wash cars."

"You'd rather ride around in cars," Jay says.

"Right," she says, thinking about hosing him down

again. "Royce Eburt's Porsche would fit me like a glove."

She and Linda decide they'd like a couple of Sno-kones from the Sno-kone man over in the flea market. I volunteer to go get them a couple. They aren't carrying money. The rich never do.

I take my time rambling through the flea market. Since they pack up before I'm off work, I've never been to it before. It's a scene all right, like a tacky carnival. All sorts of weird wares laid out on car hoods, under awnings, on rickety tables. Aged ball-peen hammers for a buck. Recycled kids' toys and tired lawn furniture. Old curlicue black walnut tables with cracked marble tops. Whole basements cleaned out and priced to move.

The sun's merciless, turning the asphalt under our feet into black Jell-O. There's a line of people with small kids for the Sno-kone man, and I join it. It creeps forward, while I'm trying to decide about flavors.

Edging past a card table full of an amazing variety of stuff, I draw in an elbow to keep from knocking down a tower of glassware.

A voice says, "You break it, you buy it."

I nearly break up the whole display. I nearly pitch forward across the card table. Because Margaret's sitting in a collapsible aluminum chair with a cash box at her feet. And she's wearing a tank top, cut-off pants, and a somewhat old-womanish type sun hat. There's suntan lotion rubbed all over her shoulders in white waves. She lifts her left arm in a slow arc and waves fingers at me. It's only quite a bit later that

I realize this is to show me that she's out of her sling.

"Margaret?"

"Matt?" She gives me an exaggerated squint like she's spotting me from some immense distance.

"What is all this?"

"This is my business. You remember barn sales? Garage sales?"

"You do this every weekend?"

"In season," she says. "On winter weekends I do my buying. In the trade we call that 'picking.' Then when the flea markets start up in the spring, I sell."

"You make money at this?"

"Eighty-five fifty today so far," she says. "Not bad."

"You got that kind of money for this stuff?" I survey the table groaning with old plates, picture frames, vintage fruit jars, horse brasses, butter molds, and a lot of items that don't seem to have any purpose at all.

"Most of my better things are gone. The dealers come around early, and they've picked me fairly clean."

"You're not a dealer?"

"I'm a *picker*. The dealers buy from me. You see that bootjack?"

I identify it only because she's pointing right at it with a finger none too clean.

"It's black wrought iron—very old. Some dealer will come along and get it for five dollars, and by Monday it'll be in an antique shop down on Wells Street with a twenty-dollar price tag on it."

"You've got it marked at ten dollars," I point out to this poor confused girl.

"That's how you price it if you're going to take five for it."

"I see." Sort of. "You like doing this?"

"I like the money. Did you make eighty-five fifty today?"

"Don't rub it in."

Directly behind Margaret is a giant steamer trunk, presumably filled with more antiques of tomorrow. Over the open lid appears a face, bright red. It's Jason, her stepbrother, sweating up a storm in a damp polo shirt.

"Hey, Margaret," he says right in her ear, "you want these cowbells out?" He rings one, also right in her ear.

She closes her eyes. "If they're priced, Jason, you can put them out, and we'll give them a try."

"Right," he says, a bustling little businessman, disappearing back into the trunk to root out more merchandise. He barely notices me.

"You've put Jason to work?" I say to Margaret, amazed as usual.

"He needs an occupation. He even likes it."

"I thought maybe you—liked to keep your distance from him."

"Once I've staked myself to a college education, I'll be getting away. Until then it's easier to deal with him than to avoid him."

"Do you pay him?"

"You better believe it. He's not the volunteer type."

"I think you like him," I tell her.

She smiles, wrinkles up her nose. "He's not a bad kid if you keep him busy."

I should be moving along. I've already lost my place in the Sno-kone line. But it dawns on me—maybe for the first time, maybe not—I don't want to leave her. "I was just over there, helping out at the junior-class car wash."

"You were?" I seem to surprise her with this evidence that I'm rejoining the human race. I decide to surprise her again.

"We're raising money for the junior dance. Will you go to it with me?"

Yes, she's surprised, or something. I tense up, waiting for an answer to the question I didn't know I was going to ask.

"I'm sorry, Matt. I can't. It's the same night as the senior prom."

"And you're going?"

"I'm a senior. You think I couldn't get anybody to go with?"

"I think you could do anything you wanted. I just wish—"

"I'm going to the prom with Joe Hoenig."

A picture of hulking Joe in his towel floods my mind. "You know Joe?"

Her eyes are enormous. "Yes, I know Joe. I go to school with him. I go to school with *you*."

"I realize that. You've got to overlook this—fog of self-pity I go around in all the time. It obscures my vision. Are you and Joe an . . . item?"

"We just both happened to be free on prom night. Actually, I doubt if I'm his type."

"Margaret, you're not a type at all."

"Thank you very much. By the way, are you interested in the bootjack? I can do a little better on the price."

"Are you kidding? Oh, I see. I'm taking up your time."

"Well"—she considers—"it's possible there are paying customers out there. Besides, the Sno-kone man's about to close up for the day."

"Right. Just answer me one thing. How come every time I see you, you seem like a different person?"

She scrunches up oiled shoulders. She puts her head on one side, cocking her crazy hat. Her expression seems to say that this is one thing she can't answer.

I'm the Sno-kone man's last customer. And while I wait for his wares, I realize I'm in love with her. I'm in love with Margaret. It'll never work. It's not even right. I don't *have* the right. I once told a girl I'd always love her. And now I love Margaret Chasen, and I don't even dare say I'll always love her. But I always will.

The car wash seems to have worked through its customers. I hand the melting cones to Linda and Carol. And while Carol tries to stuff syrupy ice down Todd's Northwestern University T-shirt, I find myself alone with Linda. We're both a little quiet. Linda usually is, and my mind's still over there someplace in the flea market.

"Matt," she says, "I suppose you weren't thinking about going to the junior dance."

113

"No, not now."

"I was sure you wouldn't be," she says in the kind of voice you use at a funeral. "I told Carol so."

Linda's being very thoughtful, and she's making me feel very guilty.

"We've decided," she's saying, "all of us—we're not going to the dance either. Carol and I decided not to, and Jay and Todd agree."

With only half my mind functioning, I get her drift. Dory's group has decided to honor her memory by staying away from the dance.

"Anyway, it wouldn't be any fun without her," Linda says.

"And yet you're helping raise money for it."

"Well, we all thought we owed that much to the rest of the class."

I stand there, in no particular world. The flea market's breaking up. I'm acutely aware of vans pulling out, tents coming down, merchandise being stashed away for another day.

"Don't you think we're right, Matt?"

"What? Oh, I guess that's your way of dealing with the situation. To tell you the truth, Linda, I haven't found any workable solutions for myself. Dory's beginning to fade for me. I can't remember her face. Not missing her is about as bad a feeling as missing her. I'm somewhere between grief and guilt, if you want the truth."

Linda, a good listener, works her hands together, almost wrings them. They're long and snowy. The bones in them are bird-fragile.

"I understand," she says. "We've talked a lot about you."

"But not to me."

"I'm trying to now, Matt," she says in a voice I hardly hear.

"Did the others tell you to?"

"We all decided. We're going to get together on the night of the dance, just the four of us. The five of us if you'll come. It's not a party or anything. It's just being together. Carol thought of it, but we'll be at my house. How does it sound to you?"

Morbid. Worse, a nightmare. The five of us—no, the four of them and me, trying to turn the clock back. With Linda getting more and more unsure of herself and Carol getting more manic. Then I try to picture what I'll be doing that night by myself, and it doesn't look a damn bit better.

"It sounds fine, Linda."

Chapter 13

It's over a week till Linda's nonparty. Plenty of time for me either to back out or develop a reasonably positive attitude about it. As Linda would say, I owe them that.

Around school I only catch long-distance glimpses of Margaret. Maybe I don't know what I'd do if I saw her nearer, though I figure out where her locker is and happen to drop past one day. But all I see is Joe Hoenig's broad back where he's propping up the wall, waiting for her.

Then that Saturday night arrives, and Glenburnie's alive with seniors heading off to the prom and juniors who've given the gym a sudden disco disguise. The spirit of John Travolta is abroad and stalking the suburbs. I'm in my room, getting ready to make a return to Glenburnie Woods.

I pull on the Lacoste shirt Ron convinced me to buy

when they reduced the price twice. I think of taking a pin and picking the alligator loose to pass the time while I wait to be late.

Out in the kitchen Gram and Dad and Beth are setting up a card game. I wander out on my way to the car. The three of them are at the kitchen table, and Gram's giving the deck a professional shuffle. She's out for blood. There's a small pile of dimes in front of each of these big-time gamblers.

"There you are," Gram says. "I was just coming to get you. It's more fun four-handed."

"Going out, Gram. Sorry."

"Oh, well, if you're going to be that way about it, I won't have a chance to take your money." To Dad she says, "Cut the cards."

"Matt," Beth says, "you look nice."

Gram looks up. "He sure does. He's got a real manly figure if he just wouldn't go around in that sloppy sweatsuit thing."

I jingle my car keys and swell up my chest, trying to make my alligator wink at her.

"We're not going to get a call on you in the middle of the night from the Evanston police, are we?" Dad asks, pretending to be intent on scooping in his cards.

"You hush." Gram slaps at his arm. "Don't embarrass the boy."

"I think we can all anticipate a quiet evening. I'm just going over to Linda Whitman's." I say this mainly to hear the sound of it myself.

"I bet she's a real nice girl," Gram says, drawing an ace.

"I don't know any other kind, Gram, but I'm looking."

I leave them laughing. I should stay home; they're planning to have a good time.

Linda Whitman's house is, if anything, bigger than Dory's. It crouches on the heights of Glenburnie Woods with one wing almost on the country club golf course. There's a white gravel turnaround in front, and Todd's Triumph and Jay's spidery black Corvette are nuzzled into the smooth green wall of a curving hedge.

Mrs. Whitman answers the door. Linda's the only one of the group whose parents stay home when she's having people over. We'll have the family room to ourselves, but there's the controlling presence of parents only a couple of blocks away in the living room.

She leads me through the house, murmuring in Linda's own voice, and gives me to Linda.

The group's clustered at the far end of the family room by the doors open to the terrace. Even before I join them, I see how I'm going to throw them out of balance, destroy their foursomeness.

Carol's sitting on a sofa between Jay and Todd, and I'm already wondering things I've never wondered. Carol relates to both of the guys, full-time. Linda doesn't seem to relate to either one of them. I don't see how they all pair off, or if they do. I could never see these people except as background characters in the Drama of Dory.

We need her this evening—bad. The small talk's very small. I ease into a chair across from Carol and

Todd and Jay. Linda hasn't sat down yet. She's surveying us, running her white hands down her sides, trying to play hostess according to her mother's rules and not Carol's.

"I don't suppose," Linda says, "Daddy would mind if we opened a bottle of wine—just one."

"Never say no to a drink," Jay remarks.

"Oh, why should we?" Carol says. "We never did —before. Let's not change." She bounces on the middle cushion of the sofa and looks at Todd, expecting him to agree. Maybe Todd's her property. Besides, the evening will get out of her control if Linda starts calling the shots.

"We've got to do something, Carol," Jay says, but she doesn't turn his way.

"We never did before," she says, getting shrill. "I mean just being together was enough."

"It isn't now," he says.

Carol looks at me. I'm the intruder. The widower returned.

"I'll put on a tape," Linda says, halfway to the cassettes before Carol stops her.

"Don't bother. That senior serenade we're getting from the club is enough sound. If you play a tape loud enough to drown it out, your mother'll be in here in a flash."

I hadn't even heard the music till she mentioned it. The seniors are having their prom at the country club, and a song—"Summer Nights" from *Grease*— is warbling in across the golf course. That should take my mind off things.

They go on bickering, and I sit there watching. I never noticed how little Carol is. Todd's and Jay's

119

knees stick far out, but her feet barely touch the floor. Everything about her is little except for her voice. Little pinched mouth in a little heart-shaped face, and little lines around her mouth, pulling tight. If she'd just relax, maybe we all could.

Jay starts prowling around the room, looking at the pictures on the walls, opening drawers.

Linda's settled beside me on the arm of the chair, though I don't remember exactly when. She watches Jay rifle the room, but says nothing. He finds a backgammon board and offers to teach Todd and Carol the game. She leaps up, ready to learn, ready for anything.

Linda doesn't move even when they set up the game at a table in the corner. "That should keep them occupied for a while," she says like somebody's mother.

She and I sit there, and I go into kind of a trance, staring out across the black golf course in the direction of the music.

"You're really quiet, Matt."

"I'm not great in social situations."

She murmurs a laugh. "Is that what this is?"

"As Carol says, 'Let's not change.' I suppose we all ought to play along. She's doing her best."

"But it's not good enough," Linda says. "The problem is, I was Dory's best friend, but Carol wants to *be* Dory."

"And she'll never make it," I say.

"No." Linda plucks at a pillow. "Come on out to the kitchen and help me find something to feed them." She stands up in one of those single graceful movements of hers and puts her hand down, pretending to pull me out of the chair.

The kitchen's gigantic, big enough for a restaurant. There's a center island with pots hanging down from above, and at least two stoves. On the counter her mother's laid out a banquet. Chips and dips, shrimp on beds of rock salt, little sandwiches with the crusts cut off, a mountain of potato salad, and a punch bowl full of ice and canned Pepsi. Mrs. Whitman wouldn't have gone for that wine idea for a minute.

It's amazing. I keep spotting more food on more mounds of parsley.

"Did you fix any of this, Linda?"

She shakes her head, and her hands move among the dishes.

"You mean your mother did all of this—since supper?"

She murmurs another laugh. Her almost white eyelashes shield her eyes. "Matt, we have a cook."

"Oh."

"Come on, help me carry things." As she glides behind me, her hand trails across my shoulders.

We set up the feast in the family room, but the backgammon players are deep into their game. I carry in the punch bowl, and we pop the tops on a couple of Pepsis. Linda drifts out onto the terrace, and I suppose I'm expected to follow.

There's a moon, white in the sky and white again in the windshields of the cars parked over by the country club. The parking lot's full. Royce Eburt's unmistakable Porsche is parked well out on the eighteenth green.

You can hear the music better out here and see the glitter of the big mirrored ball turning above the dance floor at the club. Linda settles onto the terrace's low wall. "I suppose we'll all be over there a year from tonight."

"I'd like to be there now," I say without thinking.

"You would? Why?"

". . . Because I'd be glad to be graduating."

Linda draws her knees up and almost huddles there on the top of the wall. "You're like us," she says. "All we talk about now is college. You'd think Jay was already accepted at Harvard. And Carol's going to go to Northwestern, so Todd will too."

"If Todd and Carol are making plans together, does that mean you and Jay . . ."

She looks aside and smiles. "No. Jay will go east to college after next year. And then he'll go to law school out there, and then he'll join some big firm and marry the boss's daughter."

"Do you all have the rest of your lives mapped out like that?"

"I don't," Linda says. "But then, I'm always looking back. Probably because all the times we had with Dory meant more to me than to the rest of them. You can understand that."

The moonlight's on her face, and there's a tear in the corner of her eye. She makes herself smile again. "Everything reminds me of her and those days," Linda says. "Once we were out here on the terrace— dancing around, acting silly. And somehow we broke one of the panes in the window. Just a little one, down low. I guess we were only in sixth grade, and I was terrified.

"But you know Dory—she always had a plan. She jumped right over this wall and started running all around the golf course like mad, and of course I went along. She was streaking through the sand traps and poking around in the rough. I couldn't figure what she was up to, but finally she found a golf ball somebody had lost.

"She grabbed it up and raced back to the house with it. Then she went inside and put the ball right down on the rug beside the broken pane. The minute she did it, I realized it was brilliant. It looked just like some golfer had knocked it through the window. Of course we went off then and played upstairs the rest of the day.

"Mother never mentioned it, and I think Daddy was completely fooled."

Linda clutches her knees and rocks back and forth a little like she's laughing silently. But the tear is down on her cheek now.

I'm standing over her, casting a shadow. I'm expected to do something now, but the music from the prom's flooding my head.

"Stay with us, Matt," Linda says. "Be one of us."

"Linda, you better not speak for the others."

"Why shouldn't I?"

"Because I don't have that much in common with Jay or Todd. And Carol doesn't really want me around."

"I do. Doesn't that count? And not just because of Dory." She huddles even more, and it's an invitation. "I want you for myself. You don't even know how nice you are. I like you better than . . . anybody."

The light from inside the house falls across the

123

terrace in long yellow squares, and the music from the club never lets up. The backgammon game's winding down, and the players are finding the food.

"Let's go inside, Linda."

She waits a moment. Then she swings her legs off the wall, moving like she's tired, and stands up beside me. She'd be almost my height if she'd look me in the eye. But that's another thing I don't want.

We join the group, who are piling food on plates. Carol pretends we were never gone. "You've thought of everything but silverware," she says to Linda, who darts away to the kitchen like a—frightened deer.

And then I make my move, while they're dipping shrimp and ladling out potato salad. I don't pick up a plate. I don't dig in. I walk around the table and stop between Todd and Jay.

"Listen, guys, I've got to be going." I even clap them both on the back. "Good to see you."

"You're leaving?" Jay says. "Where you going at this time of—"

And then Carol catches his eye, and he clams up. I catch hers. "Good night, Carol."

She looks up and then down. Her shoulders shrug —only a twitch. The coward in me wants to leave before Linda comes back. But no, she's back already, moving silently across the floor.

"I've got to go, Linda. You want to walk me to the door?"

The silverware rattles in her hand, but Carol takes it from her, frees her to see me out.

We walk through the quiet house, and when we get to the front door and freedom's in sight, I turn to her.

124

"It would never work, Linda."

"I don't see how you could know that, Matt. You won't try."

She reaches out to touch my arm, but she doesn't cling. "I suppose you'll go on thinking we all looked down on you. Just remember I didn't."

"I'll remember," I say, moving away from her. I'm outside, but the door doesn't close behind me. She's standing there, just a step above me, and says, "Seeing you go doesn't seem right. It doesn't even seem loyal to Dory."

I turn back at the bottom step. "Dory's dead, Linda."

The way the El Camino's parked, it blocks the drive for the Triumph and the Corvette. Maybe I knew all along I'd be leaving first. The engine starts at a touch, and the car crunches away over the marble-chip gravel and out onto the smooth curve of the street. But I'm not halfway down the first rise before I swerve into a parking place, bump a tire on the curb. I'm not ready to go home. I've got unfinished business, if I can only figure out what it is.

I yank the emergency brake, kill the lights. Then I'm out of the car, locking it up, breathing in the first real lungful of air this evening. It's just lightly scented with apple blossom.

I climb back up the street, hearing the wind high in the trees and seeing, over the Whitmans' roof, clouds crossing the moon.

If I can find a way up past the house without stepping on the crunchy gravel, and if I can find the way through to the golf course . . . I take it slow and amble along past the garage, not caring to be shot as a burglar, not now.

And then I find it between two big snowball bushes. The golf course opens out in front of me, miniature hills rolling toward the country club. I break into a run across a smooth green and up a graded hill, losing no power on the rise. My feet find their pace, and I hit it. Lord, I can't even remember when I ran last, but it feels great. I head for the music.

Chapter 14

And don't stop running until the long windows of the country club throw their paned light out onto the grass around my feet. I stand there, gulping air, but not from the run. Through the windows pinkish light drops in diamonds from the mirrored ball. The seniors in their private world.

I wonder what I'm going to do, because this next part could be tricky. They're coming to the end of a slow dance now, and they're all white dinner jackets and swaying skirts and flowers.

This is insanity. I could be arrested. For trespassing. For being a junior at the senior prom. For wearing a Lacoste shirt to the wrong occasion. They could throw the book at me. The floor's clearing out, and couples are moving in toward another room. The diamonds of light fall on polished floor. I step just inside.

And see her then, at the far end of the room. Joe's

with her. I've never seen a dinner jacket that big. He's rubbing his knee—the bad one.

She's wearing a formal. Naturally she'd be in a new disguise. She has a million of them. Tonight she's passing herself off as the most beautiful girl in the room. The light makes her dress pink, and the flea market's made her bare shoulders brown. She's this totally unapproachable creature, laughing at something Joe's said, or just at Joe.

There aren't many people in the room now, except the three of us. If she'd just look this way, she'd see me. Of course, as long as she doesn't, I'm safe, if that's what I want.

But it's Joe who spots me. He raises a weight-lifting arm and points a sausage finger at me. I shrink, just a little. They're starting across the floor, my way. Margaret's wearing very high heels. Joe's limping, and they keep getting nearer and nearer.

I start chuckling when they get into range. I jam casual hands into pants pockets. There must be a way of carrying off this situation if I can just come up with it.

"Matt?" Margaret says.

"It's Moran," Joe says. "I told you it was."

"Hello there," I say in a voice I've never heard before. "I just happened to be in the neighborhood, and . . ."

"Man, what are you doing here?" Joe rumbles. He's an incredible sight in formal wear, and I think the bow tie under his concrete jaw is the clip-on type.

I slip my hands out of my pockets. If he should decide to deck me, I don't want to be found on the floor with my hands in my pockets, for some reason.

"Joe, I don't think I can explain." I glance at Margaret, but she's just looking very attentive.

"Try," says Joe.

"It's this way." I clear my throat to go on. "I've been seeing this girl. You know—around. Off and on."

Margaret's mouth begins to twitch.

"A senior girl?" Joe wonders.

"Right. A senior girl."

"Good for you," Joe booms. "I remember that little talk we had down in the locker room. You ought to be getting out and circulating again."

"Yeah," I say, barely audible.

"But, man, what's your plan? You figuring on abducting her from the prom or something?" Joe looks baffled, and big.

"Well, Joe, I didn't have what you could call a plan. But what you suggest doesn't sound too bad."

Margaret's looking at the ceiling now, smiling wildly, her chin quivering. I only catch a glimpse of her out of the corner of my eye.

"Who's the girl?" Joe wants to know. His hands are on his hips, and he's the picture of confusion. The carnation on his lapel looks like a pinpoint.

"Well, the thing of it is, Joe—it's Margaret."

Her head drops forward. The orchid Joe's pinned to the strap on her dress nuzzles her chin.

He turns her way in slow motion. "Margaret?"

She points unnecessarily to herself, nods, and makes her biggest eyes yet—right at him.

"Margaret?" he says, thrusting his head a lot closer to me.

I nod, somewhat hopelessly. "The thing of it is, Joe—I'm pretty crazy about her."

He blinks. "You're crazy all right."

I'm thinking, hard. My head's cracking open with the effort. "Joe, what would you say if we just got out of here?"

"Who? You and her?" He jerks a vast thumb at Margaret, who stares at it in fake amazement. Oh, yes, I know her. She's getting an enormous charge out of this whole thing.

"Well, no," I tell him. "That might be pushing things too far. How about the three of us just . . . going someplace?"

"You mean you and Margaret, with me tagging along as a—whaddaya call it—a chaperone?"

"You'd be great in the part, Joe."

But he doesn't hear this. He's turned to Margaret. "What do you think about all this?"

She bites her lip, throws her eyes around, gives it some thought. "Well, the thing of it is, Joe, if you push me around that floor one more dance, I could be crippled for life."

"You?" he says to her. "Do you know how my knee's hurting me? It feels about like it did that time they carried me off the field in the Glenbrook North game. You know this prom could cost me the Heisman Trophy?"

"And the evening's young," Margaret reminds him. "After the prom there's the senior breakfast. You know we have to stay out all night. It's tradition." She chances a glance my way.

Joe's eyes are bigger than Margaret's ever get. "All night? Cheez, I can't stay up all night. I'm trying to get back into training. When did they start that tradition?"

He's not as astounded as he's acting. In fact he *is* acting. "Where'd you think the three of us might go, Moran?"

"I don't know. Up to the lake, maybe?"

Margaret's grinning now, and nods just once.

"What lake?" Joe asks.

"Juniper Lake."

"Never heard of it."

"You'll love it. It's only about an hour's drive."

"I'll sleep in the car," he says, then adds, "I've got to get out of these shoes." He lifts up a foot to show us a patent leather shoe. About a size fourteen.

Then we three are strolling off across the golf course, away from the light. Margaret's heels sink into the turf, so she slips her shoes off and carries them. Joe's shoes are already off, and he's trudging along, glad to be free of the prom. He plucks off his bow tie and flips it far into the dark.

We detour around the Whitmans' house, and then Joe says, "Say, Moran, you remember that girl I told you about, the one who goes to Maine Township? The one I'm always hanging around looking for?"

"I remember, Joe."

"Well, if it was that girl you were after and not Margaret here, I think you should know I would really do you some major damage. In fact, you'd spend the rest of your life trying to breathe through your belly button."

"Right, Joe," I say.

"Right, Joe," Margaret says.

Since there's no back seat in the El Camino, he

has to ride up front with us. Margaret's wedged between us with her big skirt billowing up. And before we hit the expressway, Joe's asleep, and snoring.

She and I don't say much. It's a beautiful night and an open road. I could make it up to the lake in forty-five minutes, but what's the hurry? These seniors have to stay out all night anyway. It's tradition.

Just after midnight we're on the road past the riding academy fence. The road's a tunnel through the trees now, and it all smells like summer already. An owl swoops low ahead of us, his claws just skimming the headlight beams.

" 'The woods are lovely, dark and deep,' " Margaret murmurs. She's been dozing, but she's coming around.

"I know," I say.

"That's a line from a poem—Robert Frost."

"He's right."

We dip down toward the lake, and you can sense the water somewhere ahead. Branches brush the fenders. Then we pull up in the yard in front of the cottage. The engine's been Joe's lullaby, and when I switch it off, he's suddenly awake. "What's that?" he says, flailing around. "Where are we?"

"We're here, Joe," Margaret says. "Get out of the car before you batter me to death."

His puffy eyes look past her at me. "You got a bunk here? A cot or something, because I am really bushed, man."

"Right up there on the porch, Joe. I sleep out there

132

all summer. You got lake breezes and the birds for an alarm clock."

"Good," he grunts.

We're out of the car now, and the stars look close enough to touch. They're always like that up at the lake. Joe's stumbling up the cottage steps, but he thinks of something and turns back to us.

"Say, Moran, you remember that girl I told you about, the one who goes to Maine Township. The one—"

"Yeah, Joe, you told us."

"I did? Oh. Well, keep it in mind." And then with a casual pile-driver hand, he sweeps the screen door open.

And Margaret and I start down to the lake, with a few stars through the trees to guide us. My hand finds hers, to show her the way. From down on the pier we're going to have a great view of the sunrise.

ABOUT THE AUTHOR

Richard Peck is the author of *Secrets of the Shopping Mall* and *Are You in the House Alone?* (available in Laurel-Leaf editions). His novel for adults, *New York Time*, was recently published by Delacorte Press. He lives on Candlewood Lake in Connecticut.

Laugh. Cry.
Be scared.
Beware.
Behold!

YOUNG Love®

IS A VERY SPECIAL FEELING

Judy Blume

Judy Blume <u>knows</u> about growing up. She has a knack for going right to the heart of even the most secret problems and feelings. You'll always find a friend in her books—like these from Laurel-Leaf!

Beverly Cleary

WRITES ABOUT TEENAGERS AND FALLING IN LOVE!

____**FIFTEEN** $2.25   92559-2-35
When 15-year-old Jane Purdy meets Stan Crandall, new boy in town, she knows he's everything she wants in a boyfriend. But the course of young love never runs smoothly!

____**JEAN AND JOHNNY** $2.25 94358-2-26
It's downright embarrassing how 15-year-old Jean Jarrett acts because 17-year-old Johnny Chessler thinks she's "cute." Eventually she returns to her normal state—and to a hard-won independence.

____**THE LUCKIEST GIRL** $2.25 94899-1-22
Spending junior year with her parents' friends in California—going to a different school, meeting new friends—changes Shelley's life. So does falling in love with Hartley.

____**SISTER OF THE BRIDE** $2.50 97596-4-47
Sixteen-year-old Barbara MacLane helps her older sister prepare her wedding, surviving many comic crises along the way!

LAUREL-LEAF BOOKS

LAUREL-LEAF BOOKS

FIC
Pe

Peck,

Close Enough to ch